The Formula

by

JJ Keller

Men and Women of Valor

The Formula

Cover Art by *Lea Schizas*

The Wild Rose Press, Inc.
PO Box 708
Adams Basin, NY 14410-0708
Visit us at www.thewildrosepress.com

Publishing History
First Edition, 2025
Trade Paperback ISBN 978-1-5092-6201-4
Digital ISBN 978-1-5092-6202-1

Men and Women of Valor
Published in the United States of America

Dedication

For Elizabeth Clester, because we share countless wonderful memories. Thank you for being part of my story.

Prologue

McCartney evaluated the situation; the ending might be gruesome. Joe and Nick had gotten creative with a torture contraption meant to kill. Within minutes Nick wrapped her into a type of straitjacket, leaving the cocoon open at the top. He strung her from the rafters by a braided rope which burned into her wrists. Below her toes, a board rigged to a crossbow would fire a very sharp looking arrow. If her grip on the rope slipped, her feet would touch the board releasing a missile. The harness kept her body aligned. She couldn't sway or swing her legs enough to clear the deadly trigger. Even if it were possible, her dismal upper body strength quickly faded.

"It's the terminator, a four-point tip on a steel shaft loaded onto a highly sensitive crossbow." Joe's smirk emphasized his recently fingernail-scratched face.

"Yeah, pointed right toward the red bull's eye," Nick goaded. He lifted his arm and pointed his gun fingers straight at her heart.

If she got out of this mess, she'd enlist in a weightlifting program. Maybe she'd ask Molly to go with her to a fitness center. Her weak arm muscles vibrated, bunched and jumped. Despite the frigid temperature, sweat beaded on her forehead. A couple of blinks helped to eliminate a sweaty droplet.

She tried to wrap the rope around one wrist but bungled the attempt and the pungent hemp grew slick.

Her feet lightly brushed the wood. She moved her fingers higher and tightened her grip on the cord. How much longer could she last? *Stop! If I lose hope, and my grip, we'll die.*

Chapter 1

Where it began…

The earsplitting quadruple knock woke her. Her overly large cellphone blinked, indicating a warning. She jumped from the sofa and glanced at the security panel. A man shadowed the paned window. Her heart palpitated to an uncomfortably fast beat. He pressed the video doorbell.

McCartney James ducked, scurried across the planked floor. Bent, she edged along the wall toward the door. "Coming."

She glanced at the display screen again, unbelieving of who stood on her cottage porch. With a total of three hours of rest in the past two days, she didn't want to entertain company, especially a well-dressed illusion. Maybe she was having a fantastic sleep-deprivation hallucination, complete with a man in costume. She pushed the speaker icon. "Yes."

"I'm from the Coterie nation, endorsed by your friend, Forest Dog. I need to talk to you."

"What?"

"We want your help."

She keyed the alarm code, tugged the door open eight inches and blinked. His incredible golden colored skin appeared to be smooth, while his repellant frown a complete turnoff. Owl feathers plumed from the band around his bulging upper left arm. His hairless muscular chest coveted a red and black beaded chest plate, and his right arm had three magenta slashes. He looked authentically familiar. Had she had this dream before? If she controlled the figment, could she change his snarl into a sexy grin?

"McCartney James, you must come with me." His rich deep voice met her expectations.

She chuckled. "Usually, I don't travel in my dreams."

He took a step back and inhaled. "Lady, this isn't a dream."

Realization struck her like a blast of frosty Indiana snow, not a dream. A Native American in full regalia stood in her doorway. She retreated and prodded the door shut with her barefoot. "I need to go. I'm expecting the sheriff any minute to go over some disciplinary actions for gangs in the community—in a previous life I was an attorney." Sleep babbling was something new for her.

He grabbed the door handle and halted the action. A small smile tightened his stern face. The guy must have asthma as he took a second deep breath. "Ms. James, my name is Seattle Coyote and I'm here on behalf of the Coterie Nation." He paused for a heartbeat. "Please come with me to the village to talk to the elders."

By his snarly facial expression, the word "please" had been forced from his mouth. She choked back hysterical laughter. If he assumed she'd simply get in his car, he was insane.

"I won't go with you, a stranger, to this mystery village." The low sun indicated night would fall and darkness terrified her. Evilness exists and spreads depravity through the black of the night, even in a B+ crime rated city. She shoved her hand against the door.

"I'm not at liberty to give you all the details. I've a letter from Chief Hawk of the Munsi tribe for you." He reached behind his chest plate and extracted a sealed envelope. "They recommend you contact young Forest Dog, anytime. He wants you to help us."

She took the paper, flipped it, and viewed the seal. Official in appearance, fifty arrows, rainbow lines, horse, cow and sheep, corn and mountains. "What can you tell me?"

"My village has been in existence since the late 1850s. When our forefathers were forced to give up their land and relocate to reservations out west, some tribal members from various nationalities came to settle in southern Indiana. The lands are owned by the clan. Enough background. The elders found some merit in your exposé, regarding the spiritual leader, and they want you to tutor one of our members to pass the bar exam."

"Law? Native American law?"

"Yes, law. Public."

"You've done your research, so you know I'm not practicing, and I'm not a tutor?" She broke the seal.

"The council is aware of that."

"So why do they want me?"

"You'll need to ask them about their reasoning." Light-footed he rocked between the porch and her entryway. Not a single board squeaked under the weight.

She removed the letter. "What was your name, again?"

"Seattle Coyote."

She recognized Hawk's writing and stepped aside, allowing Coyote to enter. He followed her into the kitchen. A motion sensor light flicked on. She flipped her hand over and back to indicate for him to sit. He tugged a chair from the table and sat, the trouser fringe stringing along the edge.

The document appeared to be authentic. She'd partnered with Hawk for a year, creating a manuscript. An innate trust developed as they worked on the production, and he'd mentioned his cousin, C-Eagle and a quest. If Hawk needed her assistance in tutoring a law student, she'd provide guidance. In the letter, he explained the tribe had an important journey and the outcome would be extremely valuable to Native Americans in general.

She was curious about the quest. In her new line of work, she needed inspiration. If she went to a hidden Native American village, she might get the motivation to create a documentary.

"Ok. I'll go with you, but I must be back in two hours."

"What about the sheriff?"

She rolled her eyes, slipped on running shoes and removed a lightweight jacket from the closet. While putting it on, she slid pepper spray and a taser into her coat pocket. "Did you bring a change of clothes?" She didn't believe his frown could get any more disgusted looking. "Insult?"

He didn't respond.

She held open the door and nodded. "Just thought you might be more comfortable with your chest fully covered." She set the alarm and followed him onto the porch. "Where's the car?"

"Horse is faster."

A man of few words. Twenty minutes into the ride she asked, "My bum is a little numb, how much farther is it?"

On a horse, behind a virile Indian, the rising and lowering on the seat in one of her screenplays may have been a sensuous scene but in real life, not very pleasurable.

"Do you always complain this much, Ms. James?" He didn't trouble himself to slow the gallop.

The wind blew his headdress, tickling her nose. She sneezed into the groove of her arm. "Please call me, Mac."

"Mac." Quick and precise.

"Seattle, if I remember correctly, means man of high status. What is your role in the tribe?"

"Messenger."

"Generally, I'm very patient and considerate of others, but I'm on the backend of a horse. And you're a rather large man, so you take up quite a bit of space. Why couldn't you have brought a mount for me? Better yet, why couldn't we add a few minutes and use my car?" She shifted on the warm leather.

She patted the sweaty coarse hair of the horse, creating a scented wave of equine, mixture of hay, oats, leather, and the outdoors. "No offense to you…ah insert horse's name."

"Cotton Ball," man of high status replied. "Shorter by horse. It's not much farther." He halted the beast on top of an incline.

She glanced around the hunk-of-fun's broad shoulders. They were at the end of the trail and below, in the valley, nestled a twilight hued village.

"Shangri-La," she whispered.

"Excuse me?"

"It looks like Shangri-La in the book *Lost Horizon*, a perfect city located in a perfect valley, where beauty surrounds the people. I cannot believe we're in Indiana."

The panoramic view had beige capped foothill ranges in the background. Limestone and clapboard houses formed a semi-circle. It appeared as if they had solar shields installed for power. The blades of the large windmills squeaked and added an ambiance to the naturalness of the setting. Somewhere in the distance the soft roar of water tweaked her auditory senses. Maybe hydroelectricity provided an additional source of the faint evening light visible through the windows of the houses.

The grass was an astounding vivid emerald. Full grown brown and dry barley or soybeans bent in the cool fall wind. Distant mournful ululations of cattle echoed from the outlying areas. Her father would have wept at the ecologically sustainable environment.

One of the long fox tails from Coyote's headdress blew back into her face and snapped her out of the trance. For the first time since the journey initiated, he turned in the saddle and stared.

"From your reaction it's obvious that you appreciate the ecological sanctity we have in the village. Maybe the elders knew what they were searching for, in you, McCartney James." He resituated, kneed the mount, and they trotted into the center of the hamlet. He stopped in front of a round building. "We can go in now. The elders are waiting."

His voice and demeanor were different, more relaxed. He dismounted and extended his hand. The warmth he evoked went directly into her palm as she slid from the horse. Seattle held the door, and Mac viewed the tribal council members. Not one of elders, wizened old men, smiled. The multitude of furrowed skin gave them the appearance of Shar-Pei dogs.

Each councilman was dressed in unique Native American garments. The pungent odor of the authentically preserved leather made her appreciate the ornate simplicity of the ceremonial dress and want to barf at the same time. Their beaded finery had different Native American symbols stick drawings, such as deer, arrows, women and men. The colors, azure, maize, ochre, greens were rich and gleamed in the soft lights. They'd brought their formal attire, which meant they wanted something significant. Probably more than simple tutoring, perhaps something she couldn't provide.

She crossed her arms in front of her and glanced at her jeans, paint-splattered cotton shirt, and scuffed stained sneakers. A bit intimidated, she smiled and cleared her throat, then lifted her chin and feigned a confidence she didn't feel. "Gentlemen! I understand this honor and respect you're awarding me. Please help me to understand why I was requested to appear in front of you." She gazed into each set of eyes of the twelve men seated at the horseshoe shaped table.

"Ms. McCartney James. We're privileged by your kindness and generosity of time. We'll explain. Please have a seat." The oldest Shar-Pei indicated one lone empty chair. She glanced around; her escort had disappeared.

"I'm C-Eagle. Because of your association with Forest Dog and Hawk, we value your skills. We request you tutor one of our tribal members. He must pass the Indiana State bar exam to help us with a crucial quest."

"What is the quest?"

"Not necessary for you to know."

"To recap, you want me to help a young man pass

the bar exam, but you won't provide why the outcome is so important?"

"Yes."

"I don't have any skills in teaching, and I haven't practiced law in a year or more."

"We'll provide the tools." C-Eagle stood. "You'll be here every Sunday morning from eight to noon."

"What happens if I agree to help tutor…"

"Caedmon Star."

"And he doesn't pass."

"He will."

She nodded. "On Sunday I'll evaluate Mr. Star and decide if I can assist."

As if timed, the members stood. The door opened and in the fading sun the outline of Seattle filled the twilight lit space.

"We will see you soon, Mac James." C-Eagle bent his head.

Dismissed, she contemplated what they weren't saying. Why the grand ceremony for a simple request?

For the return trip, Seattle provided a second mount. "Thanks for the horse, what is his name?"

"Midnight. I borrowed him from one of the guys."

"That was quite a session with the elders. Why were you so mysterious at my house? What is the big secret they can't share with me?"

He'd changed clothes while she'd talked with the council. His chambray clothed back did not twitch. No sounds were forthcoming. The only movement was a gentle nudging of his booted feet to the sides of the white horse. Had he heard her? People complained about her soft voice.

"You're not very talkative, are you?" she shouted.

No response.

She gave up and rode in silence the rest of the way. When her sweet little cottage came into view, she couldn't help but smile. Set in the woods with the tiny porch off the back door, the house provided everything she wanted in a retreat. Her father's influence for a love for ecology and conservation brought her to this remote setting. In his memory, each day, at sundown, she'd go into the peaceful forest and absorb creature noises and conjure the sublime elements of nature. Upon dismount, she felt the soreness of her inside thigh muscles. She regained control of her legs, walked to Seattle Coyote and handed him the reins of the black horse. "Thank you."

"You'll keep the horse to travel. We'll provide food and straw for Midnight. We'll ride together. Be ready at seven." He handed her the reins and continued, "You apparently have some knowledge of horses. Do you need me to unsaddle and comb him down?"

"Yes, thank you. It's been a while, so run me through the routine." They moseyed toward the barn. "Since you're in the talkative mood now, I'm assuming I was the chosen one for this tutoring experience because of my brains, right?"

"Not to insult you, but because of the exposé about the Native American Activist Forest Dog. Your sympathetic honesty appealed to the council. Also, location."

"Right. Location."

He quickly and efficiently dismounted, allowing the reins to drape over Cotton Ball's sides, then slid open the barn doors. Stale hay odor permeated the air.

"Part of the reason I love this parcel of land is

because of the barn. I had envisioned transforming it into a creative arts workshop. Now it's going to be used as a horse hotel."

"Huh." He grunted and led Midnight into the first stall. "Do you have grooming tools, specifically a brush or towel to wipe him down?"

"Don't know; I'll look inside the groom's closet." She found a small door and within a few minutes located an old brush with slightly flattened bristles. "Here is an adequate brush. I'll go in the house and get a towel. Be right back."

She ran into the kitchen, gathered a couple of towels and returned to the barn. He'd removed the saddle, blanket, and then the bridle. He talked her through each step. Her gaze followed his gentle lean hands. Rolled shirt sleeves exposed hairless muscular forearms as he brushed the horse. "Will you look for a bucket to put water in?"

She hurried from the barn and returned with an oval metal container. "Why did you name a warrior horse Cotton Ball?"

"My niece named him. Since he's all white, she thought he looked like a big wad of cotton. It stuck."

Within a few minutes, he'd completely brushed and rubbed the horse down with the towel. All the while, he used his velvety voice to soothe the animal. "You are the greatest beast ever to take on the task of transporting a complaining woman for many miles."

"Thanks," she muttered, making sure he caught the umbrage. Midnight snickered.

Seattle took the container and went outside. He seemed to know his way around. Putting the pail of water in the stall, he sauntered in his light-footed manner into the courtyard, grabbed the reins off the ground and mounted Cotton Ball. "Thanks for helping my people. See you on Sunday."

Not one iota of sincerity came from those perfect lips. "Oh, thank you, but I can travel to the village and back by myself."

He lifted an eyebrow.

"I'll use my car." She pointed to the off-road vehicle five feet away.

"Horse. I'll see you Sunday."

Chapter 2

Robert Barringer slid from his truck. A woman, having crested the hill, stopped her jog a couple of yards from him. Her chest expanded, as if capturing as much of the clean sweet air as possible. Pine trees overpowered the little daisies and wildflowers edging the deer path to her left. Was she staying with McCartney James?

He contemplated waiting for her and introducing himself, but a horse's pain-filled whinnying came from the open barn door. Rob stepped into the stable and waited for his eyes to adjust from bright light to darkness. A second later he smelled her, a mixture of sweat and a spicy citrus scented perfume.

"Hi! You must be the vet, I'm McCartney James. As you can see, I called you because he has a limp. Maybe a hoof problem. I searched the net and concluded a vet was needed." She talked fast, and her hands fluttered.

"Hi. Unusual name." Rob should have asked his boss if the superstar neighbor was a man or a woman, with an old chap's name he'd assumed. Even the county courthouse clerk said his new neighbor was an ugly gray-haired bossy New Yorker. Robin Dick needed to have his eyes checked, beautiful didn't describe her. Early to mid-thirties, he wanted to remove her hair thing and run his fingers through those blonde strands. Her gray-blue eyes reminded him of a summer day beginning to cloud up for a nice warm shower. She wore exercise gear with a logo, resembling a bird, on the jacket. He exhaled and bent over the horse hoof. A job was a job.

"Yep. Family name. My dad tried to get all his relatives in one swoop. Love the relic 350 truck, blue is my favorite color." She pointed to the horse. "So, what's your professional opinion?"

"A typical problem for this fella." He released the front leg, straightened and faced her. "I'll show you where the problem lies."

She inched closer to the horse. Rob lifted the rear hoof and outlined the infected area. The shy gelding, Star, bolted sideways. Mac, hurled backward, collided with the barn wall. "Ouch."

Rob dragged himself from the straw covered floor and went to her. "Are you okay?" He took hold of her arm.

"I think...I'll be fine. I seem to have been pierced by something." She bent her head to peer over her shoulder. "I'm stuck."

He pulled her jacket away and evaluated the situation. "A rather large nail. I'll get you released. It's going to hurt, but I'll make it quick. First, I'll help you remove your jacket, so I can see how deeply embedded the nail is and the angle."

She grabbed the front of her jacket and clinched the stretchy material tight to her chest. "Not necessary. Can't be that deep, please help me disengage." She extended her hand. "Pull."

Rob caught her silent accusation. Evidence: she was suspicious. "Hey, I'm trying to help."

She twisted, glancing over her shoulder. "I guess an animal doctor is an MD, so it'll probably be like you're inspecting a horse." A grimace scrunched her face, then she pushed a strand of hair behind her ear.

"Um, I usually don't compare women to horses." What could she possibly have to hide under her jacket. He debated telling her he wasn't a vet, but would she allow him to help her? In addition, she presented a pretty package on the outside but what about underneath the garments. Images of a gross scar or abnormal malady like a skin disease or an exposed extra nubbin raced through his mind. Regardless, Valor expected him to protect her and so far, he was failing at that role.

"Sorry, PTSD." She unzipped the jacket, slowly, grinding each metal tooth.

He averted his gaze from her exposed upper body and assisted her with the sleeves. Like driving by a car wreck, you prefer avoidance but it's impossible not to stare. She wore what looked like a sling shot, the cotton or spandex crossed the back of her neck, and the binding surrounded and lifted her well-endowed attributes. She stiffened. He expelled a breath and shifted his focus to her face.

"What's wrong? Is it serious?" she whispered. Her milky white skin had a pearly sheen and glimmered in the dim light.

He tipped his hat farther back on his crown. "No, I think if I push forward on your lower back, you'll be released. It'll cause you a bit of pain and your um, garment will be ruined, but you'll be free."

"Ok, I'm ready whenever you are." She started to breathe with a rhythm, deep inhale through the nose, exhale out through her unusual mouth.

"I'm going to stand in front of you and reach around to pull you forward." He encircled her shoulders. His upper body and her soft endowments came together like the opposite ends of two magnets.

Due to her earlier apprehension, he was suddenly supersensitive. "This is going to be awkward, but I need to get closer to you to get a good grip." The contact of his chest to her breasts made his breath catch. *Good God.* "Ready?"

She shut her eyes. "Yes."

Hunched over, he exhaled. Mere inches apart their faces could brush, skin to skin. He employed all his military training to restrain, to not caress. She had an amazing mouth with a plump top lip, much fuller than the bottom, making it appear as if bee stung. He wanted to taste, to suck, to ease the imaginary sting. Get a grip Barringer and focus on helping this poor woman.

Her head touched his chambray shirt, and hot puffs of air heated him. "I'll make it quick, so it'll be over in a few seconds." He flexed his biceps, drew her forward and tugged. Freed, he held her close. "Are you okay?"

"Yes, fine," she whispered

"Turn around and let me see the damage." With a tender nudge he brought her about and saw the blood running along her concave spine.

"Well?"

"It doesn't look bad, but it's bleeding. We should probably go into the house and clean it with soap."

"Hi, Rob, and Ms. James I assume."

Rob pivoted. Mac peered around him. At five seven the newcomer, Joe, was the same height as Mac. His black hair, parted on the side, had a few pieces falling onto his forehead. Silver graced his sideburns and above his ears. He winked as if knowing he'd interrupted a moment.

He extended a hand. "Dr. Joseph Fox." His shiny

onyx eyes glittered. "I'm the veterinarian. I believe you called me, to look at a horse. Rob, it's good to see you. Have I arrived at a bad time?"

"Hi, Joe. How're you doing?" Rob wrenched her jacket free, covered her front and proceeded out of the stall.

"Not bad for a weekday." Joe gave a quick perplexed glance at the equine. "Isn't this Marcus's horse?"

"Who's Marcus?" Mac's narrowed eyed stare hinted at her displeasure.

"Marcus is my son." Rob glanced at Star. "His horse was stolen two years ago."

"Since you aren't the vet, who exactly are you?" The chill in her voice should have started a snowfall inside the barn.

"I'm your neighbor. Rob Barringer, here to help." His smile broadened. He removed his cowboy hat and performed an exaggerated bow.

Her mouth gaped open. "Mr. Barringer, although I thank you for assisting me in getting extracted from the nail, I don't appreciate your humor. You knew I assumed you were the veterinarian, and you let me continue to believe it."

"You believed what you wanted to believe. If you had inquired if I was the vet, then I would've told you."

She turned, holding her jacket like a shield, and stormed toward the open barn doors.

****

"Mac." Rob's laughter came out in waves.

"Ms. James, to you, sir." She tried to make the sir sound like asshole and stomped along the path to the house.

"Even after what we've been through together?"

She stopped at the entrance, firmly planted her foot, pivoted, and glared.

"Ms. James, then. You'll probably want to have a physician look at the injury, and if you haven't had a tetanus shot in the past five years get one." The odious man grinned.

"Ms. James, please allow me to look at the injury." Dr. Fox lifted a medical bag.

"Thank you, Dr. Fox, I'd appreciate your professional evaluation." The words dripped from her lips sweet as sugar. First, she'd get a look at his medical license.

"Well, I guess you two are sparking. And since you're my friend, I'll tell you up front, I'm going to add wind to the fire." Joe grinned, stopped beside Mac, and they entered the cottage.

Mac turned from the window, holding the coat to cover her less than perfect body. Anger rushed through her. He should have said something. Dr. Fox placed his old-fashioned black leather bag on the table. "Sorry, not to trust, but could you show me some identification?"

He removed a couple of licenses from his wallet and held them out. "Ms. James, since the puncture is low on your back it would probably be a good idea and remain at the window. It's always best to get additional direct light for ministrations."

"Please call me Mac, Dr. Fox." She glanced at the IDs then through the pane. Rob Barringer led the horse from the barn. The jerk. How dare he mislead her?

"Call me Joe. I'm going to turn you sideways, to get the best view. Visibly it is quite deep, about one to two inches. Fortunately, it doesn't appear as if an artery was punctured. I'm going to clean the area with alcohol, which will burn." He removed a long cotton swab, the length of a ledger page, from the bag and dipped the tip into a bottle of pungent rubbing alcohol.

At the sting of the antiseptic, she clenched her teeth and counted the seconds.

"I admire your stamina. You didn't flinch." She ignored the rustling and concentrated on the liar outside.

Rob walked the horse toward the broken-down corral. She didn't want to repair the fence, because she had no intention of using it; however, the corral added quaintness and another layer to the forest scenic view. In the mirror reflection of the windows, she noted Joe bending over her backside.

"My mother believed if she blew on the injury then the antiseptic wouldn't hurt as much." Paper flapped and the breeze did cool the sting. "Do you jog often?"

"Three or four times a week. Not a fan, but I do love chocolate. I can't have one without doing the other, it's all about balance."

"I agree with Rob, get a tetanus shot. When was the last time you had one? I'm putting iodine on the puncture."

The stinging returned. "Ah, when I was twelve. Didn't really care for it." She hissed through clenched teeth. "That…hurts."

"Do you have a physician in Lantern?"

"Not yet."

"If you want, I'll call a friend, Noah Worth's a medical doctor, and see if he can get you in today."

"Thank you, Joe, I'd appreciate it." She hesitated. "The horse was a gift, so I don't have paperwork. I'll pay for treatment though, and Rob can take him to his son."

"That's right neighborly of you, Mac. Hey, we've a community barn dance to raise money for the football team on Saturday night. Do you want to go with me? I'll introduce you to some of the townspeople." He'd packed up his gear and held the bag as a shield in front of him, giving her an impression he expected a refusal.

"Sure, I'd love to go with a new friend to a local fund raiser."

He smiled. "I'll give you a call to arrange a time." A few minutes later she strolled with him to his vehicle. Rob led the horse near them. "Mac said you could take the horse home with you and give him back to Marcus."

"Mac, is it?"

She caught Rob's slit-eyed glance and in response she spread her five fingers and pounded them to her heart. "A horse should be with its true owner."

"Where did you get him?"

She shrugged.

Joe glanced between them. "Help me load Star onto my trailer, and we'll take him to your house."

"Thanks Joe, I appreciate it. I'll have Closs treat his injuries. I think we've the meds; unless they've changed."

"No, they'll be the same." Joe glanced at her. "I just got a text from Noah's office; he'll see you today. I'll send you the address and time."

"Thank you."

They finished loading the horse. Mac waved at them. "Good day, gentlemen. Thank you, both, for your assistance."

"My pleasure." Rob waved toward her backside. "Sorry about the misunderstanding."

Joe tipped his hat. "I'll see you on Saturday."

Mac walked into the house, locked the door and set the alarm. In the bedroom, she selected clothes and headed toward the shower. Part of the reason she exercised was to avoid physicians, and yet she'd get a needle stuck in her bum. In retrospect she should've evaluated the faded red barn, before housing the horse. Six months ago, she'd purchased the cottage. Tired of pavement, tall buildings, and the constant congestion of New York, she needed a retreat. Most of all, getting away from him was vital. She shook her head. She wouldn't let that evil man distort her thoughts.

She'd found the perfect setting to provide many years of inspiration for her writing. In addition to real life scenarios, the nature surrounding the house would provide dangerous twists of fate taxing her heroines and inspire the heroes to rescue her. Maybe she could convince the council to let her make a documentary about their journey. What was their quest? Could she convince Seattle to give her information? Showered and dressed, she grabbed her car keys, purse and headed out.

Mac drove along crooked country roads toward I 64, and into the quaint town of Lantern. She lowered the driver's side window, allowing fresh fall air inside. Her dark shaded sunglasses fogged in the humidity. She laughed aloud. Her ex-boyfriend told her at their parting, "You can take the girl out of the country, but you can't take the country out of the girl." He was right, she enjoyed living in quiet serenity. She shook off the chills. Could she develop agoraphobia?

She'd chosen Lantern, Indiana due to their fiercely independent multi-cultural people who spoke their minds and took care of their own. Tourism wasn't a thing in Lantern and the townspeople seemed to want to keep the no crowd philosophy. On the fence, she wanted Lantern to be prosperous, but also for it to remain caught in that old-fashioned time warp. Clark Street was lined with shops authentically restored with distinctive gray slates, and original colors of rusty red, deep blue and forest green. The center of a roundabout had a grassy area complete with a white-washed gazebo, making the town movie-set ready.

The local governing structure, strongly supported by the ties between the individual and the state, facilitated open debates and gossip. A blessing or a curse, everyone knew something about everyone; how else would little Tommy have been rescued from the raging waters of the Ohio River if it wasn't for the town crier, Sam Martin.

She arrived at the address Dr. Fox provided. The red brick building's architectural detailing drew an eye from the long-arched windows to the buttress at the top. Sunrays sparked off the slate roof. She parked her car and walked toward the black door. It opened from within and an older lady with short, silvery-gray hair and black horn-rimmed glasses bustled from the office.

"Hi. How're you today?" She widened her smile. "Great day to be outside." Without waiting for a response, in a flurry of movement she rushed along the sidewalk.

Mac grinned and continued inside. At the desk an ebony-haired curvy woman searched through a file drawer. "Just a second and I'll be with you."

Mac waited, appreciating the tasteful contemporary decoration of the reception area.

"May I help you?"

"Yes, thank you. I'm McCartney James. Dr. Fox called to see if I could get a tetanus shot."

"Oh, yes. I've some forms for you to fill out, and then you'll see Dr. Worth directly." She turned on a banker's lamp and continued, "It looks like it's getting gloomy outside. You look familiar, do I know you?"

"I don't believe so, I'm new to the area. What's your name?"

"May, May Fox."

"Are you related to Joe?"

"Yes, my brother. We both chose the medical field. My job just happens to be regular hours." She handed over a clipboard loaded with pages. "I'll also need to copy your insurance card and driver's license."

Mac extended the required cards, then sat on a periwinkle blue chair. Several pages and minutes later, she gave the completed forms to May. She nodded. "Looks good. A few minutes and Dr. Worth will see you."

"Thank you, Ms. Fox."

"Call me May." The desk phone buzzed. "He's ready, please come this way."

The only accents in the room were old fashioned apothecary jars. Everything else, including the paper covered examining table, was top of the line medical equipment.

She hoisted herself on top of the parchment covered bench and waited, dreading the needle. Dr. Worth walked in reading papers on a clipboard, no doubt reviewing her medical history. He was beautiful, no other way to state it.

He put the clipboard on a nearby desktop and extended a hand. "Ms. James, I'm Dr. Noah Worth. Nice to meet you." The man had a six-foot frame and perfectly cut blond hair. His bright blue eyes showcased crinkles at the corners giving his features an appealing charm.

"Nice to meet you, Dr. Worth."

"It appears as if you were punctured by a rusty nail earlier today. Please let me see where the wound's located?"

"On my lower back."

Dr. Worth lifted Mac's blouse and removed the bandage. "I'll just call in the nurse, and we'll get this treated." He pressed an intercom button located on the wall, then went to the sink and scrubbed his hands. As he put on sterile gloves, May entered the room.

"Nurse Fox will get the inoculation prepared. Please remove your blouse. I'll put a topical numbing agent on the area and pry around a bit. After cleaning the puncture, Nurse Fox will give you a tetanus vaccine, maybe a prescription for antibiotics, and you'll be good as new." He flipped on a lamp and pointed the heat toward her backside.

"Do you want a smock?" May asked.

"No, I'll be fine." She sucked in her breath and straightened her back.

"Ah, it looks rather deep, but the opening is already closing. You'll feel a cool numbing around the area."

May swabbed Mac's lower back.

"I'm just going to probe around a little to see if any rust decided to cling to the inside. If the exploration becomes uncomfortable for you, please let me know and I'll use an injection to numb it."

No way. Mac twitched and stiffened. "I'll be fine."

The doctor touched her shoulder. "I need to clean a small portion a little deeper. Are you doing okay with the pain?"

"A little prying is much better than needle sticks any

day."

"Thata girl." A few minutes of additional ministration, he finished. "May will put on a bandage, then we will get to the good stuff."

"Good stuff, such as?"

"The shot. Your paperwork indicated your fear of needles, Ms. James."

"Mac. I'm not a fan, but I know it's necessary."

"I wish all of my patients were this considerate." He chuckled.

May flicked the prepared needle. Mac's body psychologically tensed. The injection wasn't as painful as she'd expected.

Minutes later, Mac walked a few steps to a new bookstore called Books and More. A clever logo of a book with glasses sitting on the cover made her smile. Doorbells announced her arrival. She inhaled the fresh scent of the newly issued books and magazines, enjoying the libraryesque aroma. Reds, blues, blacks, the hard back and soft cover books, offered a sensational journey which would never end. Organized and tidy, with a pleasant mix of genres, would meet a variety of taste and reading needs. Newspapers were at the front of the store, fiction on one side and non-fiction, autobiography on the other side. Colorful printed matter, stacked on tables, would temp any youthful shoppers. Comfortable looking easy chairs invited the customer to sit and browse a piece of history or fiction.

"Hi, I'm Molly Black. Welcome to Books and More. May I help you find something?"

"McCartney James. Yes, I'm thinking of refurbishing a barn and wanted to see design books if you have any." She couldn't pull away from the section of

Gardening with Ponds.

"I have a limited selection on this table." She pointed to a group of hardbacks next to Mac. "You may be able to find somewhat outdated titles at the library on Clark Street." The shopkeeper moved a few feet and rearranged the literature.

Mac snatched two gardening softcovers from the table and glanced at Molly Black.

"Oh my, God. I cannot believe it's you. I was just putting a poster figure together of your recent adventure movie, *Red Hot*. It's in the back room. I cannot believe you're in my bookstore. Oh, MK, sorry, Ms. James, may I, um have your autograph?" Her hands flapped, and her perfect little mouth moved non-stop.

The lovely petite woman reminded Mac of the little pink bunny on television commercials advertising batteries. She had straight heavy auburn hair; the shiny locks were pulled back and held by a clip. Azure eyes peered from behind the clear lens of her glasses.

"Ms. Black."

"Please call me, Molly."

"I'm Mac. I'll be more than happy to give you an autograph."

Molly ran to the back of the store and hauled a large cardboard figure of a Native American out to the main hallway. It depicted the elder Forest Dog to the finest detail, from the multi-colored headband around his long black hair, to his bulging bicep muscles, including the loin cloth covering some of his spectacular muscled thighs. Xavier was successful in perfecting the display, correctly illustrating this famous Native American.

Contract signed; the movie would stream later this year. A romantic suspense, created from the documentary, contained facts about the Native Americans struggle to preserve earth and the balance of nature. The publicity about the exposé helped to advertise the movie and no doubt had prompted Seattle Coyote, and party, to shanghai her.

"Here's a permanent marker. If you wouldn't mind signing on his marvelously well-developed chest...plate."

Mac chuckled and took the pen. She almost signed McCartney James but readjusted her thought process and wrote MK across the poster.

"There you go. Molly, I love your store. Your sections are well designed, and the subjects are diverse."

"Thanks. Literature's my passion. I especially like to have children come here on Saturday for story hour. The library does a similar thing, but their story time is after school." She set the poster against the wall. "Do you live in Lantern now?"

"Yes, I bought the Carpenters' place. I met Liza in the St. Louis airport. I was going to South Carolina, and she was headed toward California. We both had layovers, and one thing lead to another, ending with me convincing her to allow me to look and possibly buy her house. Six months later, here I am."

"Welcome to Lantern." She lowered her glance. "Would you be interested in meeting for lunch sometime next week?"

"Yes, I'd like that. Will Tuesday work for you?"

"Great."

They chatted for a while longer, about various subjects. "I need an outfit for a barn dance. Do you know of a place I could get something to wear?"

"Yes, a local vendor of western wear is on Main

Street. Bell's." Molly pointed to the right.

Mac nodded. "Will I see you at the football fund raiser?"

"Yes, we are strong supporters of the school corporation." Molly smiled. "Do you want to buy those books?"

Mac chuckled. She clutched two gardening books, a restoration paperback and Midwest-living magazine. "Yes, please."

She drove to Bell's Western Gear. A sales associate, dressed in a fringed vest and skirt, helped her locate the women's section.

She tried on numerous outfits and decided on a slinky dark gray tank top and black jeans, secured by a concho-link belt. A deep brown wool-lined suede jacket and slouch leather cowboy boots completed the outfit.

Later that evening, she put on the boots and ambled, trying to adjust to the creaky new leather. Examples of popular country line dances were easy to find on her laptop, and she turned up the volume. Her feet crossed and she fumbled, finally she got the country version of a grapevine when a message appeared from Xavier.

—*How R the Boonies?*—

—*Great! How R U?*—

—*Not well. Dumped.*—

Mac thought of Dr. Worth.

—*Normally sad about that, but I met someone who is a perfect match for U.*—

—*DETAILS.*—

Xavier replied.

—*Tall. Built. Handsome. Good sense humor. Dr. Noah Worth.*—

—*What's wrong with him?*—

—Nothing. Perfect. Maybe not out.—

—Now tempted. When should I expect delivery of the new script?—

He sent a sigh emoji.

—Do you have anything written?—

—Yesss, I'll have the first five scenes by the end of next week.—

It was a stretch, but she had a feeling the story would quickly unfold.

—Didn't you put the first word on the page yesterday? I guess you really don't want to go back to the old days of litigating contracts or whatever boring tasks an attorney does. Hey, gotta go.—

—K. Night.—

She shut down the laptop.

New York had so many activities; numerous eateries, abundant shopping, and the theatres, but she believed she'd stay happy here. Where else would a cute little old lady greet her on the street like a long lost relative?

She glanced at the rear entrance door, locked. Outside the kitchen window, she noticed a flicker of light, near the hot springs, then the flash extinguished.

Chapter 3

Rob repeated the three knocks on the solid oak door. Her car was in the drive, but she could be jogging. He walked to his truck to get a pen and paper to leave a note, when the high-pitched sound of a female singing shattered sound waves.

He pinpointed the origin of the screech and strolled around the side of the house. Instead of an angelic voice, his neighbor had a warble. Earbuds, the white ends barely visible under the baseball cap, short sleeved shirt, and athletic shorts with a pocket for her cellphone, completed the image. She picked up small stones, transferring the rocks from one pile into what would be a natural wall for the hot springs pool. The gray, cream and brown cobblestone background of the grotto, with steam rising in front, provided a serene setting.

"Hi, Mac," he shouted. She jerked around, her face paled, and skittish eye movements made his heart thump. "I'm sorry; I didn't mean to scare you." To expose his face, he tilted his fitted cap.

She removed her gloves, pried the earbuds free and sat on a pile of stones. "I wasn't expecting anyone." A touch to the cellphone and the rock music stopped. Her hands shook as she untied a bandana from around her neck and wiped her face. "I thought I'd take advantage of the warm weather."

"How is your wound?"

Hands clasped; she glanced at the boulders. "Good. Just a little stinging."

"I'm glad. Good idea to enjoy the Indian Summer; cold sets in fast in this area." Rob sat beside her and extended a bunch of flowers. "For you."

"Thank you, Rob. They're beautiful." She held the bouquet to her nose. The lilies mingled with the herbal scent of the woman.

"As are you." He smiled at her lopsided grin.

She eased the floral stems into a wooden bucket full of water. "Daises, miniature sunflowers, carnations, white lilies, tansy, and fern leaves, all my favorite flowers." She quirked an eyebrow. "Looking at social media?"

He pulled the hat bill lower on his forehead. "I'd never admit to that. Some of them are from my garden. It's my way of apologizing for yesterday. I didn't intentionally mislead you. Everything happened so quickly."

"I did assume. You were kind enough to help me, and I treated you horribly. Did Star have any injuries from being in the stall?" She met his gaze dead-on. Not bashful, she would be a force if attacked; however, he wouldn't let that happen.

"No, he's fine, thank you for asking." He removed his hat, cooling his crown. "To further the apology, I'd like to ask you to go to dinner tomorrow night."

She moved a strand of hair, tucking it under her cap. "No further apologies needed, but I'd like to go to dinner with you."

Rob replaced his hat, a nervous gesture he couldn't seem to lose. "You're creating an attractive landscape, want some help moving the stones?"

"It's very sweet of you to offer. I might stop for the day." She wiped her hands on the kerchief. "Do you think I could use the springs like a hot tub?"

He didn't like the clenching of his stomach muscles. To ease the discomfort, he rolled his sleeves and walked to the pile of stones near the house. He picked up several and carried them to the pond. "I'm not sure about the depth, but it's natural. It must be deep enough to be fed by underground aquifers. I know the conservation officer, Sam Goodnight. I could have him check it."

"Thank you; I'd appreciate that."

In companionable silence they relocated cobblestones. Afternoon shadows invaded, but not before they'd fashioned a half wall. A few more rocks and she'd have complete privacy.

They sat together on the bench. He rubbed the little bump on his nose, just below the apex between his eyes, then took off his hat and laid it beside him. He used his shirt sleeve to wipe away forehead sweat.

"Did you happen to notice a dark area in the water?" She shivered. "A dead critter?"

"Can't say that I did." He glanced toward the swirling waters. "Show me." He replaced his hat, and they walked around the boulder wall to the front of the hot springs and peered over the edge. She'd raked the debris away. The sun cast a shadow on the water but didn't reveal an animal.

"I don't see anything, but that doesn't mean it isn't there." He tipped his hat back and peered into the murky abyss.

****

Mac hated rats and rat-like creatures. She glanced at the Blue Mountain Pine tree, her point of reference, and drew her glance back to the springs. She took his hand, walked a few feet to the left of where they were standing. "Right in here. Dark, large, hairy."

"I need to stir the water. Will you hand me the rake?"

"It bobs." She handed him the tool.

"Will you hold my hat?" He extended the cap "What's with the stare? Is there a hat ring? Can't be helped." He pushed a hand through his wind-blown shaggy hair.

His gorgeous blue eyes burned into her soul. "No. Yes. Um, I think you're very hand—dy to have around." She took the hat and held it close to her midsection.

"Right. That's what all women say." He dragged the rake through the water. A few muck-drenched leaves came from the depths.

"Go out a little further."

"Take hold of my hand."

She placed his hat on the nearby bench and grabbed his hand with both of hers. He scoured the basin, dragging the dark waters.

"Did you get it? It is a rat?" She bit her lower lip, planning to bolt the moment the furry creature came on land.

"No, I think it's bigger than that." Rob extended out as far as possible. She followed, moving closer to the edge, and braced her feet. He drew the rake. "Don't let go."

"Don't worry, I won't let you fall." She set her back teeth and hung onto his wrist.

On firm dry ground, he set the wood rake handle on a rock. Hooked on one of the prongs was a blob, skimming the water's surface. "What do you think it is?"

"We need to call the sheriff." He extracted his cellphone and punched numbers. "Hey, Langley. We've a body at Mac James's house. Yes, the Carpenters' old place. No. No ambulance is needed, just the coroner."

Her heart slammed into her chest. A body bobbed in her hot springs. "If the man or woman had been murdered, how cruel to toss him or her into hot water." She tried to look at the corpse.

"Yes, nasty soup." He refused to move. She stepped. He stepped. She tilted to the right; he tilted to his left. "You don't need to see."

"Okay, I'll get a couple of bottles of water." She rushed into the house, washed her face in the kitchen sink and grabbed water bottles from the fridge. Other than wine, she didn't have alcohol, so nothing stronger.

He took a long drink of water. "Stop it." His short terse statement threw her off guard.

"What?"

"Please stop humming the theme song from that cop show. Those refrains aren't right for this." He waved toward the body.

"Oh. Sorry. I deal with stress through sarcasm or humor." She glanced at the pond.

"I noticed." He nodded toward the house. "Have you seen anything unusual?"

"Last night. A flicker of light, but it quickly disappeared." She lifted her cap and scratched her head. "Do you think this happened last night?"

"No. I lost a calf once and two months later we found it in a hot springs. It had similar decay, so probably didn't happen last night."

"So, this person was dumped in the water about the time I moved into my perfect retreat."

He frowned, then glanced at the lane. A brown and cream Sheriff's car stopped a few feet away, then a big and tall cop got out of the vehicle and meandered toward them.

"Rob. How are ya doin? Miss, I'm Sheriff Langley Simpson." The angular man had a slight rounding belly, which seeped over his basket woven belt loaded with keepers. He'd unsnapped the gun protector when he got out of the car. The handcuffs were safely stored in the large case sitting on his bum. With a spare cartridge, he was equipped for most circumstances.

"Langley. How's Donna?" Rob's hand was pumped like the handle of an old rusty siphon.

"Good. She wanted me to ask if you're going to the fundraiser?"

"Yes. The football team will be outstanding this year. The specs are in, and it looks like we might have a good chance at the regional." Rob ran his hand through his hair and looked around, no doubt searching for his hat.

Langley's mouth ballooned from side to side as if he packed tobacco and needed to spit the wad. "With Marcus and Langley Jr. at the front line, I'm sure we'll get there." He drew out the sentence as if it were the gospel.

"As long as they have a good time. We found a body in the hot springs." He pointed toward the grotto.

The Sheriff touched the brim of his hat with his two fingers and walked toward the water. The body, the part exposed anyway, began to dry. "Well now. The coroner is on his way and will be the final judge. However, I can tell ya right now this man is Darrell Carpenter."

She gasped. "Darrell Carpenter, the previous owner

of the house?"

"Yes, I guess we better find out where Liza went after she sold the homestead. Damn, he owed me fifty bucks."

"How do you know it's Darrell?" Rob asked.

"Darrell was in the navy during Desert Storm. He has a distinguishable," Sheriff Simpson gave a sly wink, "tattoo on his neck."

The coroner arrived as Langley related his third historical football memory. Dr. Tom Ballard declared the body to be Darrell Carpenter, inconclusive until tests had been run, but he knew Darrell's tattoo as well. The corpse was bagged and moved to the coroner's van. Within two hours, the body and all legal parties were gone.

"I'm sorry this happened to you. It seems as if your last couple of days have been packed with unusual occurrences." Rob grinned, showing one tiny dimple on the left side of his face.

"You only know the half of it." She sighed.

"Do you still want to go with me tomorrow? I'll understand if you don't." Her shy neighbor sifted from one foot to the other. He'd retrieved his hat and currently twisted it around in his hands.

"Sure. Where are we going?" She wanted to take a shower and relax. "So, I know how to dress."

"There's a winery about twenty minutes away, Wynncliff Vineyards, which has a four-star restaurant. I thought we would go early, take a tour of the facilities and dine."

"I've been to a vineyard in Italy but didn't take a tour." She grinned, tilted her head and half-closed her eyes. "Are you trying to romance me, Rob Barringer?"

He stopped twisting his hat and inched forward. "You're an enticing delightful petite package, Mac, who wouldn't?"

Her heart beat a cadence to match the caw-caw of the blackbird flying overhead. This man tangled her insides, a twisting that she hadn't felt for so many years. "I'm up for the challenge."

"Why would it be a challenge?"

"A man hasn't been truly successful in romancing me for eighteen years." She lifted her gaze and felt a jolt.

****

"Well then, the quest is on." He replaced his hat, nodded a good-bye and trotted toward his truck. Rob turned the key, elevated the AC then selected Vince's contact.

"Bolton's Valor Security and Investigations." Vince Samuels, his former Captain, answered.

"Hey. You have a minute?" He rubbed the two arrows, an insignia medallion he kept on the key fob.

He could imagine Vince's face forming a misshaped smile. "Only a minute. Met Mac, have you?"

"I hear the laughter in your voice."

"You should've asked for details. Instead, you dove in." Deep rusty chortles came from his Army buddy.

"I thought the subject I was assigned to protect would be a grumpy old man, and I didn't want to commit. Not to mention this is the first time since she died that I've considered going into the field."

"You shouldn't give your unfaithful dead wife a second thought. Are you going to stay with the mission?"

"I can't believe how much I'm enjoying this operation. Yeah, I know she's easy to look at, but she is extremely…interesting."

"You're infatuated."

Rob laughed. "Not likely. All said, she does need protection. We found a body in the hot springs, outside her house, today. The guy was the previous owner, dumped there, but I've got a strange feeling. I'm enlisting additional help to have 24-7 coverage. We'll probably have to repay the favor. You okay with that?"

"Shit. Xavier was right." Vince sighed. "Yeah, we'll provide compensation. Who did you say is back-up?"

Vince's cousin Xavier was Mac's best friend. He'd hired Bolton's to keep an eye on her. The two guys must have a wager in play.

"The entire Coterie tribe, and they won't want money."

"Okay, if its legal. I've got a call. Reconnaissance is a shit storm right now; you're back on logistics after this assignment." He disconnected.

Chapter 4

Mac gave a fluff to her hair, walked through a spritz of perfume and hurried to answer the bell. She disarmed the security alarm and opened the door. From the wide-eyed expression on Rob's face, he appreciated her time-consuming transformation.

"Good God."

She bowed her head and plucked at the full skirt. "I'm glad I went conservative and selected the basic black dress."

"You look beautiful." He tugged on his tie.

"Thank you. Back at ya. I believe it's the first time I've seen you in something other than jeans and chambray. The suit is very becoming. The green shirt highlights the blue of your eyes." She blinked. "Do you want to lose the tie?"

"I'm not sure how formal the tour. The intelligence didn't provide a lot of background." He fidgeted, shifting his weight.

"So far, you're doing very well with the charm slash friendship quest." She kissed his cheek, then lifted the tie.

"Yes." He hoarsely answered. His nostrils slightly flared. She loosened the knot at the tie and pulled it free. His spice scented cologne, stirred by the action, stimulated her senses. She straightened out the tie with a snap and laid it over the back of the sofa.

He smiled and wrapped an arm around her waist. He kissed her, softly at first and then outlined her upper lip. She moaned and pressed closer.

"I've wanted to do that since I first met you." He released his hold and drew in a long breath and slowly exhaled.

"I'm all-in for doing it again," she whispered.

"If only we had the time." He grasped her hand and escorted her to the door. She snatched her bag and wrap from the entryway table as he opened the door.

"A luxury car. No truck today?"

"Barringer men take their dating seriously."

"Noted. Tell me what you do know about Wynncliff Vineyards."

"According to their website the winery was started in a professor's basement as a hobby. The grapevines were purchased in Ohio and shipped down the river. When the professor changed his hobby into a business, his children stomped the grapes with their bare feet."

"That's sweet." She moved the seatbelt and twisted around to face him. "A family that stomps together stays together."

"What?"

"You know, keep the family close by doing events together. When I was growing up my family always had Sunday dinner. You could miss any other event during the week, but that meal was required. What about yours?"

He sighed. "When I was young, we would play games, have a movie night, and take trips. We did that sort of thing. No group stomping."

"What about now?"

"Just me and my son. We spend as much time

together as possible considering he's a senior in high school." A lull followed.

Mac kept her silence, trying to decide what to talk about next. "Is this the place?"

"Thirty acres of lush vegetation, fences filled with grapes." He parked the car. They studied the plain unimposing winery buildings in front of them.

"Very few vehicles are in the car park. The restaurant is good, right?" Through half-closed eyelids, she connected with his blue-eyed glance.

The slightest hint of a grin appeared as he rubbed his earlobe. "Hope so, guess we should go." He clasped her hand, and they went into the main entrance of an A framed-styled building.

"Mr. Barringer?" asked an older woman, sporting long belled earrings. The janglers touched her shoulders, chiming as she moved. White short-cropped hair contrasted sharply with her flowing gypsy blouse and long skirt.

"Yes. I'm Rob and this is my friend, Mac."

"Welcome. Your private tour guide is Andrew." The earrings jingled as she walked to the reception counter and pressed an intercom. "Andrew, front." She pointed toward the north side of the building. "It'll be a few minutes, please feel free to browse the gift shop."

"Mac?" he asked. She nodded. The small well-lit room was filled with a variety of wine related merchandise. She held up a t-shirt with a logo, *A good book, a dog to nestle with and a glass of spirits is all I need*.

She lifted a bottle of red wine tucked in a bed of raffia on top of a barrel. Shouts bellowed in the corridor. She glanced at Rob, and he tilted his head toward a doorway three feet away. Posted above the door was a sign indicating employee entrance.

"I'm fired?" A man's angry high-pitched squeal drew closer.

"Yes. It didn't work out, Roger." Another male voice, with a lisp, calmly replied.

"Why?"

"A tour guide should communicate with the customers. You left out the process. As a mechanic, your fixes failed." The word, should, resonated like sssshould. His lisp revolved around the S sound. "Now, the barrels are, well they're not right. It'll take days to undo the chaos you created. Please pick up your check in the office and leave the grounds immediately." The boss sounded tired and frustrated.

"You'll wish you hadn't fired me." Roger screeched.

Rob replaced a bottle of wine on the shelf. "Apparently this part of the tour is over."

Andrew, according to his name tag, appeared in front of them. He nervously brushed brown locks from his forehead and tucked his white shirt into his black slacks. "Welcome to Wynncliff Vineyards. I'm Andrew, and I'll be your tour guide today. You must be Mr. and Mrs. Barringer."

"Mac, and I'm Rob."

Andrew shook their hands, then they followed him from the building and along the rows of grapes. The growing process and best type of grapes were a snooze, especially when he went into a long discourse about the vineyards. Rob yawned, obviously also bored with the life span and development of a vineyard. She stifled a chuckle.

"The white and purple grapes are grown on slopes." Andrew droned on about the climate of the area, the best soil, and which is why Wynncliff produces extraordinary wine. Next, he discussed the pruning of the buds to blossoms and finally the harvest.

Rob held a hand over his mouth, this time hiding his yawn. The processing of the grapes from juice to fermentation differed between the reds and the whites and the aging.

"Our job is to capture the flavors through careful and precise wine creation. Cold is used for the fermentation of fruity whites. Barrel fermentation is used for complex full-bodied whites and aeration of reds."

They were escorted to the cellars, located in a cavern with natural stone walls, slick with condensation. The wall mounted sconces highlighted and added a gloss. There were two levels of massive barrels lining the alcove. Cold chills ran across her skin. Andrew explained the difference between the French and American Oak barrel, other than color, very little deviation in the product.

They meandered toward the oak slated barrels.

"Our oak barrels come from the best coopers. It has been proven the finest quality wines are a partly due to barrel craftsmanship." Andrew tapped a French barrel, on the higher level, to emphasize his point. The earthy scent of fermenting wine and wood, in addition to his monotone drone, became sleep inducing.

"The barrels in this room have been here since 1970 at the origination of the winery. As you can see the wood is still in perfect condition." Andrew pounded the barrel creating a thunk. Gallons of pure sweet full-flavored aged red gushed onto their heads.

Rob grabbed her arm, tugging her away from the pungent purple goo. The wine continued to flow. Their tour guide stood to the side, a mere speckling of crimson on his blazer.

"Are you okay?" Rob spun her three hundred and sixty degrees, creating a circle in the rich satin covered floor.

"Yes, just a little wet and sticky. Smells good though, fruity." The wine pooled on her dress, dripping along her legs and into her shoes. "How about you?"

"Same." He ran his hand through his hair, dragging the crimson liquid to splatter. She leaned against him and emptied a loafer.

"Well, let's see how it tastes." He laughed, sucked a droplet or two off her upper lip, then jerked away. Laughter hadn't been a big part of his life the last couple of years, and this felt good.

A calm voice with a lisp said, "Sorry."

Short and pot-bellied, he rushed forward with small J-cloths in his hands. "Folks I'm sorry about this accident. Never, ever, happened before." Lisp guy dabbed Rob with a wad of cloths.

"We've a gift shop with shirts and shorts. I'll get you some clothing to wear." He held his cellphone close to his face. "No charge of course."

They changed clothes and stuffed their soiled clothing into the trunk of the car along with a complimentary case of blush wine. Red wine was too close to the moment and well, white just didn't seem right.

They sat, unmoving in the car and turned toward each other. He looked into the mirror and finger combed his wine-streaked blond hair. "Do you think we're ever going to have a normal encounter?" He winked at her, making his dimple grow deeper.

"Events take place in threes, so maybe this is the third for us. We were bumped by a horse, and I was nailed. Second, we moved rocks and found a steamed body and third a barrel of vino burst and flooded the winery. It must be the end of catastrophic events. What do you think?"

"I hope so."

"How can you smile? It has been a horrendous week so far."

"Yep, but I'm still hungry. Want to get pizza?" Could he prevent crossing the line of ethics with this mission and simply guard her?

Chapter 5

Mac's nerves jumped into overdrive when Joe Fox called to remind her about the barn dance. How would she feel being amidst so many people? She'd needed time alone, but her solitude had intensified her anxiety about being in large crowds.

While trying to decide what to do with her hair, the doorbell rang. She glanced at the camera. A smaller version of Rob Barringer stared into the monitor attached beside the door. She disarmed the system and opened the entry.

"Hi, Ms. James. Dad told me that you gave us Star. I wanted to thank you in person. Oh, I'm Marcus Barringer." He held out his slim knobby-knuckled hand.

She extended her hand. "Nice to meet you, Marcus, would you like to come in?"

"Sure."

As he crossed over the threshold, the security beeped. He looked at her with a questioning gaze.

"Don't worry, not a spy game, helicopters won't be flying in anytime, soon. This is an advanced home security and management system." She showed him the control panel by the front door, the monitors, and the back door panel. "It's highly developed. Entry can be by eye or code." The boy's mouth gaped open. "Impressive, right?"

"Miss James, what's your job, which requires a

high-tech security system in your home?" He scratched the back of his neck. His blue and white pin striped shirt was tucked into mid-washed indigo denim.

"Please call me, Mac. Nothing James Bondish, a simple writer." They had stopped in the kitchen, and she opened the glass fronted refrigerator door. "What would you like to drink?"

"Soda or water."

She handed him a bottle of water. "How about a snack? I worked through lunch, and I hate to eat alone."

"I can always eat." He stared at her. "Am I interrupting? Are you going out?"

"Not for a while. I'm going to a barn dance with Joe Fox to support the football team."

"Great. I'm going to be there. I'm a quarterback." His smile showed a slight dimple on his left cheek, making him look exactly like the guy next door.

He started forward, then stopped as if he didn't know whether to sit or stand. She pointed toward an industrial style bar stool. "Please, sit. Want a sandwich?"

"Great."

She removed two plates and prepared each serving. "How about taco chips?"

"Yes, please." He tapped his fingers on the stone countertop in a fast upbeat tune.

"Oh, I purchased a cake from the bakery in town." Within minutes they shared dip, chips and cake. Not a healthy meal, but an enjoyable refreshment.

"What year are you in school?"

"I'm a senior. Next year I hope to go to a university in Lafayette." He pointed north.

"Do you want to continue playing football?"

"No, I want to focus on my education. I'm interested

in engineering." He glanced toward the alarm box on the back door. "Your system has my interest. I like to dabble in electronics." He moved onto the coffee cake. "Did this come from Morning Bakery on Lewis Street?"

"Maybe. I don't know the town very well yet. I was on Clark Street. Does Lewis intersect with Clark?"

"Yes. I've only eaten their doughnuts, but this cake's very good."

"Thanks for the testimonial. I'll make sure I get a good supply of baked goods from Morning Bakery to have on hand. Anytime you want to visit, we'll have a snack. Maybe next time my daughter, Cassandra will be here." Mac pushed her plate away.

"You've a daughter. How old is she?"

"She's your age." Mac walked out to the great room and picked up Cassie's senior picture. "Here, this is my baby, Cassandra."

"She's pretty."

"Thanks." She replaced the photo. "She's in her first semester, studying dance, in New York."

His cellphone dinged. "That's my reminder, I need to go and pick up my date. Will you save a dance for me?"

They walked onto the veranda. She raised a brow. "Will you be able to play football with two injured feet."

Marcus grinned. "Oh, maybe I'll just talk to you then. Thanks for the grub." He waved and loped to his car.

He drove away. A midnight blue touring car pulled into the driveway. Joe wore a cobalt blue oxford shirt, gray jeans, a tooled leather belt and black boots. He removed his cowboy hat. "Ms. James, you look fabulous."

"As do you Dr. Fox. It looks as though we've coordinated our clothing." She pointed toward her gray top and black jeans secured by a leather belt.

"Yes, excellent taste. Are you ready?"

"Almost. Would you like to come in for a few minutes?"

"Sure." He walked into the main living area.

"Want to have a drink while you wait?"

"Sure. Water's fine." He paused. "Not cold."

She uncapped a glass bottle of water and handed it to him. "I just need a minute to fix my hair."

He ran a hand through her hair. "I like your hair just as it is, flowing free."

She resisted the urge to step back. "Just to clarify, we're going to this dance as friends, right?"

"That is what we agreed. However, I've the option to change your mind. I'm a very good dancer!" He wiggled his brows.

She pulled her hair into a loose knot at the nape of her neck. "We should leave. I'll just grab my purse and coat."

Mac expected a big red barn with bales of hay stacked along the side for seating. Her creative imagination could not have devised this typical North American barn with the gambrel-roof, sloping over the edge. It reminded her of the thatched roof cottages in England or the white icing perched over the edge of a gingerbread house. The light honey brown hued cedar cladding was illuminated by LED overhead lights.

Windows were placed every few feet along the bottom and sporadically on the second level. A loft held bundles of hay she'd expected to see. The sweet earthy scent reminded Mac of her childhood home. Clear decorative lights gave the appearance of tiny stars. The joist along the perimeter was painted a wheat color and had electric lanterns mounted on black forged-iron S hooks. A charming and perfect entertaining space for a retro-styled event.

Joe escorted her into a central area filled with exuberant teens. Some parents stood at the sidelines, keeping a watchful gaze. The coat-check was manned by the cheerleading squad. After handing over their coats, Joe placed his hand on her lower back and led her toward a group. They stopped near the king post, which was cleverly painted a cherry red to prevent enthusiastic dancers from running into it.

"Mac, I'd like you to meet Matt and Molly Black, Sunny and Calvin Greybird. Gang, this is McCartney James a new member of our community. She's from New York City and is a writer."

"Hi, Mac." Molly grinned.

Matt held out his hand. "Hi, Mac, Molly's told me quite a bit about you. So much I feel as if I'm in the presence of a star."

She shook his hand. "Please, I'm embarrassed. I like to write and was lucky enough to have a popular movie."

"Welcome to Lantern. Please, tell us about the movie." Sunny was a petite blonde with a charming smile and iridescent personality.

Calvin nodded.

"May I?" Molly asked.

"Yes, please." Mac glanced around the crowd as her new friend recited Mac's vitae.

She would have spotted him in a crowd of thousands. It wasn't because of his height, his wide muscular chest, nor because of his vibrant nature. No, she zeroed in on her neighbor, because of that unique connection. Maybe the draw was love-at-first sight, she'd never experienced such a strong emotion. She laughed in her head as the musicians played a sexy ballad about an incantation, perhaps that was what happened in her barn. He put a spell on her, and only time would dispense the magic.

He talked to a striking brunette with layered hair and winking diamond stud earrings. Mac squashed the illogical feeling of jealousy and shot him a smile. He nodded his head and tilted the cowboy hat. The woman said something, and Rob leaned into her. She swung her hips as she followed him. He nodded a greeting to the group. "Hello, everyone, you all know my friend, Veronica Masters. Veronica, meet my neighbor, McCartney James."

The band finished the bewitchment song, moving on to a popular melody about white trash, trailer park love. The barn's acoustics were extraordinary, as was the singer when he auditioned for a spot in the movie. "Nice to meet you."

Veronica had unusually large round eyes and a bow shaped mouth, red and rosy to match her cheeks. Mac shot her gaze to Rob as he animatedly talked to Molly's husband.

Joe shifted his hand from her waist and clasped her hand. "Want a drink?"

"Excuse me." Veronica smiled at the group. "Rob I'm so very thirsty, could we get a beverage?" She lowered her kewpie doll eyelashes over mahogany eyes.

"Sure, in a second." Rob nodded toward a stout man with long wavy hair. "Excuse me, I need to talk to the mayor."

"Excuse me, I'm going to dance with my beautiful wife." Matt put his arm around Molly's waist, and they joined the dancers.

Marcus shouldered his way into the group, towing a dark-haired female. "Hi, Mac. I decided I don't really need my toes to play ball, I toss it off fast enough." Marcus' youthful exuberance was contagious and adorable. "Dance with me?"

Mac gave a large full-of-life laugh. "Okay, Marcus, if your date doesn't mind."

The young woman behind him stepped forward. Mac held out her hand. "Hi! I'm Mac James, next door neighbor to Marcus. How do you do?"

"Oh, man, I'm sorry. This is Lindsay and—"

"Marcus, get me a cup of punch," Veronica demanded. "Please."

Marcus stiffened. "Sure. Would anyone else like a drink?"

Joe coughed. Mac glanced at him. He shook his head. "No, thank you," she responded.

The musicians ended the song. Before the youngsters were out of earshot Lindsay asked, "Is she your dad's girlfriend? She's not very nice."

"He sees her sometimes. I don't think she is his girlfriend. At least I hope not."

"Kids these days, they've so much energy." Demurely Veronica glanced at her cellphone.

Molly and Matt rejoined the group. She glanced at her friend and mouthed. "Want to use the restroom?"

She nodded. Mac whispered to Joe, "I'm off to use the restroom."

His mouth touched the edge of her ear. "Hurry back, I want to dance with you."

Rob returned with two fruit drinks in hand and reignited his conversation with Matt.

Veronica hissed into Rob's ear, "Take your gaze off that woman."

This situation was getting more embarrassing. Mac moved closer to Molly. "Ready?"

She grinned. "You're lucky. It's indoors and newly renovated by my husband." Molly looked toward Veronica and asked, "We're going to the ladies' room, want to come?"

She tossed her hair over her shoulder and literally looked down at them. "No. Go along."

Inside the restroom, Molly glanced in the mirror. "Isn't she a hoot?"

"How long have they been seeing each other?"

"Aren't you here with Joe?"

"Yes, as friends." Mac followed Molly to a row of doors designed to imitate horse stalls.

"I think they just randomly date. I don't see wedding bells in the future, unless he's a complete fool." Molly went into one of the stalls.

A sturdy metal black baked enamel bridle rack, rounded with a handle and an arched top to maintain the shape as it was fixed to the wall. Beside the sink was an antique collar, which held a roll of paper towels. The walls were painted a creamy milk color. The overall effect was inspired and charming. Mac went into one of the stalls and hung her purse on the horseshoe holder. Finished, she exited and washed her hands.

"My brother-in-law's coming the week of Thanksgiving, if you're interested in having a date you could come for dinner."

Am I coming across as desperate? "Thank you for

the invitation. I'd like to join you, not a date, although I'm sure he's nice. My daughter's going to California over the holiday break."

"Sure. I'll let you know the details the closer to the date." She smiled broadly. "I mean dinner."

"It'll be fun, and I could talk to your husband about some reconstruction on the barn at my house. I love what he did with this place. It should be in a home decorating magazine or Architectural Digest. Nice touches." Molly blushed. "You did the design, didn't you?"

"Yes, my first time. I haven't told anyone. Do you really like it?" Molly asked.

Mac grinned. "I love it. Will you help me with my barn?"

"Sure."

"Hi, girls. Oh, look how lovely this room is. I like creativity in a restroom. I'm sorry I don't believe we've met. I'm Nancy Strom and you are?" A silver haired woman widened her smile, highlighting her sparkling green eyes and mischievous persona. She extended an elegant narrow hand.

Mac clasped her hand and Nancy squeezed. "I'm McCartney James, I just moved here about two months ago. This is my friend, Molly Black."

"I know Molly. Everyone knows Molly. Where are you living, Ms. James?"

"Please call me Mac. I've moved out to the cottage on Lost Paradise Road."

"Oh. The place the Barringer family has always coveted. You must have snatched the house right away. I didn't see it on the market."

"No moss grows under my feet. I love it, and the town of Lantern. I especially like Molly's bookstore, and how well she decorated this barn. It looks fabulous don't you think?"

Nancy pinned Molly with a piercing green gawk. "Molly, you decorated the building. You've untapped talents girl. I'd love to have you come over to my house and talk to me about how I can make my family room a little more interesting. Would next Monday work for you?"

It appeared as if the chipper Molly had met her match in verbosity. "I'll be more than happy to look at your room Nancy, but I'm not a decorator. I simply helped with this project."

"You're a decorator, or at least you decorate with taste like my own. I'll see you on Monday." Nancy Strom walked into a stall and latched the door.

Outside the closed door of the restroom, they looked at each other and burst into laughter. "What a whirlwind," Mac choked out.

They were still laughing minutes later when Rob approached.

"Ladies. Is there anything I can do for you?" His facial expression resembled the one indicating I'll never understand women, which created more laughter.

They calmed and in unison replied, "No, thank you."

"Women are a mystery to me. Even after being married for years, I still don't understand their nature," he mumbled.

Mac grinned at him. "What was that, Rob?"

"I'll just escort you ladies back to the group then."

As the threesome approached the small gathering Molly grabbed her arm. "You've a daughter?"

All stares focused on Mac. Despite the wetness under her arms, she didn't flinch. "Yes, I'm the proud mother of a seventeen-year-old. She's currently attending a school for the arts in New York."

"So, James's your married name?" Molly asked.

Torrid heat rushed to her face. "No. James's my maiden's name. I've been blessed with a beautiful and talented daughter."

The silence, despite the band playing was overwhelming. She didn't want to explain her past. "Matt, I really like what you've done with this barn. When you get a chance, I'd like for you look at mine."

"Sure, Mac. I'll check my schedule and give you a call." Matt combed his fingers through his dark brown hair. His chocolate eyes looked owlish on his round face.

"Matt's extremely skilled in carpentry and construction, but he's amazingly bashful about his talent." Molly wrapped her arm around his.

"Come on, Mac, let's give it a whirl." Joe tugged her toward the dance floor. "This is a two-step dance and very easy to pick up. We'll go into the back line, so you can watch the others."

His face beamed as bright as the lanterns hanging around the perimeter. At the back of the line, she watched the woman in front of her and tried to duplicate her moves. A wave of stiffness tripped her, and she stepped onto his foot. "Oops, Joe you're going to have a sore foot later if this keeps up."

When the dance line turned, she and Joe had migrated to the front row. Veronica pushed her finger into Rob's chest. He took hold of Veronica's arm and led her into the group. People shifted, and he stood beside Mac.

Mac missed a step and crashed directly into him. As he braced her from falling, she laughed. "Mind your toes now. I don't want to injure you, too."

Near the end of the song, the routine became easier. She put some wiggle and distinctiveness in her moves.

Veronica had cleverly traded places with Rob. Mac faltered on the next chorus and caught her boot on Veronica's extended foot. Mac went flying, landing on the concrete floor.

"Oh, my mistake Ms. James. I hope you're not injured." Although Veronica's voice was apologetic, her face hinted a joyful smile.

"No, Veronica, I'll be fine." Mac braced a hand on the floor. Joe crooked her elbow and assisted her to an upright position. She brushed off the seat of her jeans. Damn viperous woman. "Maybe we should sit down a minute and catch our breaths."

He led her from the crowd and toward the refreshing air rushing in through the open door. Several benches were placed outside. She plopped onto the sun warmed surface and leaned against the backrest. The stars, beacons in the darkness, and a half-moon sprinkled limited beams. The crispness of the air helped fan her hot cheeks.

"The moon and stars make your lovely face shine." Joe's cellphone dinged, and he removed the device from his trouser pocket. "Dr. Fox. Yes, I expected as much." He glanced at his watch. "About thirty minutes, twenty at the least. Don't panic. I'll be there." He disconnected the call. "A cow's having a breech birth, and the owner cannot get it turned. You're welcome to come with me, keeping in mind it'll be a very long night, or I'll ask someone to take you home."

"You can't drop me off, at my house, on your way?"

He stood. "No, darlin', I'm going in the opposite

direction."

"I'll take her home, Joe."

She glanced around him. Rob leaned against the barn. Joe quickly reacted. "Thanks, Rob. I guess her house is on your way home. I need to head out. Mac, I'll give you a call tomorrow." He kissed her swift and light on the lips. "Um, taste like peaches."

Heat rushed to her face.

"Well, I guess you're stuck with me, kid." Rob gave a good imitation.

"Great. Thanks for the offer: however, I wouldn't want to interrupt your date with such a charming woman. I'll see if Matt could drive me home or get a valet driver." She skirted around him and headed toward the door.

"You won't be interrupting my date, but you'd be interrupting a couple's only night out in a long time." He sighed. "There isn't a taxi service in Lantern."

She stared at him, trying to decide why he would go out of his way.

"Let me take you home. I'll let you sit in the backseat instead of stuffing you in the trunk."

"Like in the movie. Funny." She wrapped a strand of hair around her right ear. "Ok, but if Marcus leaves first, I'm hitching a ride with him."

"How do you know Marcus?"

"He came by to thank me for returning his horse." She placed her hand in his and stepped over an empty soda can. "He's such a nice young man. When my daughter comes to visit over Christmas, maybe I could introduce them?" Electricity made the fine delicate hairs to stand up on her arm. She talked herself into believing the magnetism she experienced with him was in her imagination. Nope. Something existed between them.

The band played a slow song. He glanced at her. "Would you dance with me, Mac James?"

Her heart went pitty-pat. "Yes. I'd like to dance with you, Rob Barringer."

When they walked onto the dance floor, he took her hand and placed it on his shoulder, then drew her close aligning their bodies. Her two-inch boot heels brought her head below his chin. The lights dimmed, the music soothing, and their bodies fit perfectly together.

The song ended, but she wanted to continue to sway. "Thank you, sir, you're a very good dancer. Excuse me, please."

She exhaled, trying to stop her stomach from doing flip-flops and left him standing alone. The punch bowl became her target. "May I?"

"Sure." A lanky gray-haired man pulled a silver flask from his pocket. He tipped the container and glanced toward the dance floor.

She followed the man's stare. Rob danced with Veronica. Her stiletto heels gleamed and reflected the light. Mac had to admit; they looked comfortable together. The song changed to a slow ballad, a country artist. The lyrics contained the notion of a man not being committed to a woman and for people to go with the flow, simply enjoying shared time.

She turned toward the older guy and extended her hand. "Hi! I'm Mac James."

"Hi, Mac. I'm Luke." He transferred the flask from one hand to the other, to shake her hand in time with the last note.

"Here is the little tramp eyeing my date all night. Listen, honey, I want you to stay away from Rob." Veronica's stage whisper became more pronounced.

"He's mine."

Luke stepped forward. "You little snake, leave this woman alone. Your man asked her to dance. I guess you don't have him after all. It appears as if he has the good sense to be interested in Mac instead of the witch on Wall Street."

"Mind your own business, Luke." Veronica switched her glare toward Mac. "Stay away from Rob." She screeched and marched toward the restroom.

Luke handed her a cup of punch. "I think you're going to need libation if you've to hitch a ride home with those two."

She took a sip of the beverage, then drew in her breath. "What is this?" Her burning throat made her voice raspy.

"Moonshine. The finest moonshine in southern Indiana."

"I need to sit." They walked to the wallflower chairs and sat on the hard wooden seats. Alcohol? At a school related fund raiser? "Thank you, but I'm going to need earplugs and not a drink." She dumped the plastic cup in a nearby trashcan. "Tell me about yourself, Luke."

He replaced the flask in his shirt pocket and held out his hand. "Give me your phone, and I'll share my info. My grandson thinks you walk on water, and I enjoy spending time with a beautiful woman."

She handed him the device, then turned her attention to the shouting of two teenage boys. How would the townspeople deal with conflict?

"Ready?"

"Rob?" She glanced around, searching for Luke. Her cellphone fell from her lap. "Yes, let me get my jacket. I'll meet you at the front entrance?"

He handed her the mobile. "You smell like alcohol. Why?" The rebuke in his voice didn't upset her. It was a community event after all. She rarely drank alcohol, but he didn't know her.

"One sip of punch, which I didn't know was spiked."

"What?"

"Moonshine. Luke spiked my cup, and I had one swallow before knowing it was powerful and disgusting."

He took her arm and guided her to the coat check. She fumbled in her pockets and drew out the tiny red ticket, number eighty-eight. He frowned and helped her with her jacket.

Seated in the backseat, she closed her eyes wishing for teleportation.

"What's wrong with her?" Tension rolled from Veronica's tone of voice.

"She's just a little tired."

It seemed like two minutes later they pulled into the driveway of a contemporary A-frame house. The elaborate gold embossed sign indicated 909 Wall Street. "Ah, the witch on Wall Street." She giggled.

He shot her a hard glare as he got out of the car. He opened the front passenger door, and assisted Veronica, then leaned over the seat. "Stay in the car, I don't want to find you wandering around outside."

She saluted. "Got it."

"For God's sake find some mints. Your breath would kill an elephant."

She moved to the front passenger seat, adjusted the vanity mirror and inhaled. Her hair sprung out in disarray. After smoothing a few strands, she used the peach-tinted lip wand, but didn't attempt to use lip liner to balance her lower lip. A spritz of perfume refreshed her. Proper again, she popped a couple of breath mints.

What is taking him so long? Tired from an exceptionally long week, one filled with unusual events, she leaned her head against the seat headrest and reviewed each day.

****

"Mac?" Rob whispered. She snored, not the delicate wafting of air, but fog-horn snored, not even waking when he snapped on her seatbelt. He laughed and started the car. She was beautifully captivating. He understood himself well enough to know if he let her into his heart, it would be forever. He could not let that happen. Since his wife killed herself four years ago, he refused to taint another relationship.

"We're here, wake up." He tapped her shoulder.

Her eyes remained closed. "Thank you."

"Wake up. We're at your house." He ran the top of his hand across her soft cheek. "Awake, little beauty."

"Rob?" She rubbed her eyes.

"Yes. We're at your house. You'll need to enter the passcode." He walked around the car, opened the door and assisted her. Arm in arm they strolled to her front entrance.

"Don't need, it's facial recognition." She let the camera catch the image of her eye. "Sorry about the nap. I guess lack of sleep caught up with me."

"I understand." Rob once rode a cantankerous new stud, Wicked Fire, for a full thirty seconds, before he went flying. He banged his head against the hard packed soil: however, the desire to tame the stallion became all consuming. In the end, his bumps and bruises hurt like hell for several days, but Wicked Fire became docile. He told himself to relate the compulsion and uncertainty to this experience. She was a wicked fire.

She dropped her boots in the foyer and walked into the kitchen. "Do you want a soda?"

He followed. "No, thank you. Will you be, okay?"

"Sure, I'm fine, just so tired." She stopped talking and made a weird face. "Thank you for your help. I'll walk you out."

She tripped over a boot, unbalanced she stumbled right onto his chest, and they tumbled onto to the sofa. Their mouths were inches apart. His gaze met hers. She inched her mouth closer to his.

He focused on her lips, the full upper one tempting him. She shifted beneath him. He reversed positions. She ran her hands across his back and gripped his shirt. He pulled away. "Please stop."

Her body tightened. "Sorry."

"Not what I intended. I enjoy being with you; however, when we share a real kiss, you'll remember every second." He smoothed a hair behind her ear. "Good night, Mac. Make sure you set the alarm."

Chapter 6

A high-pitched buzz pierced Mac's foggy mind. Where was the doorman? She opened her eyes, *Indiana*. Her cellphone's security app flashed a red warning light. She crawled from the under the covers, hurried to the entrance and peered through the window as she knuckled the code. "Cripes, Sunday morning." Finger-combing her hair she threw the lock and opened the door.

"You were supposed to be ready at seven, and its twenty-five after. Where's Midnight?"

"Don't start with me, it has been a dreadfully long week and I've a raging headache. The stolen horse has been returned to the true owner. Know anything about that?" She folded her arms and tried to widen her sleep swollen eyes. If Seattle Coyote laughed at her, she'd punch him in the face. He quirked a small grin, wise man. She left the door ajar and walked into the kitchen, opened the freezer door. The cold air revived her. "I need coffee."

"No time."

She yawned and shut the freezer door. "Remove the hat; it shields most of your face. I can't read your expressions."

He tipped his hat and narrowed his eyes.

"Please." She prepared the coffee to drip and got two travel cups from a cupboard.

Seattle tapped a booted foot.

Mac pointed toward the counter where a leather backpack was straining at the seams. "I've gathered material. It's packed and ready to go. Let me just jump into the shower and get ready to ride. Have a seat." She waved toward the island stool. "I'll be back in a second." She spotted orange earplugs threatening to spill from his shirt pocket.

Mac, rather proud of herself for being uncomfortably doubled on top of Cotton Ball, managed to stay quiet. Seattle refused the carafe of coffee, but she'd drank hers in the first few minutes and tucked the travel cup in her jacket pocket. Awed, she viewed the quaint, yet progressive, village nestled in the center of a forest.

"What is this nonsense about the horse being stolen?" he asked.

"Two years ago, the horse, Star aka Midnight, was stolen from Marcus Barringer."

He nodded. "I'll investigate how the horse became a part of the stables."

"Wow, with all this talking I'm going to need the earplugs," she shouted. His chest vibrated; she assumed with laughter.

Seattle dismounted and held out his hand. She extended the heavy backpack, then slid from the horse.

"Caedmon meet McCartney James your mentor. Mac, Caedmon."

"Hi, Ms. James." Caedmon at five-five, with ebony cropped hair, came to her chin. His keen intelligence brightened his dark brown eyes. He wore a logo t-shirt, jeans and popular sneakers.

She followed her mentee into the same building where she'd met the council. "I've a lot of information from my book collection." The leather-bound legal books slid from her backpack; she placed them on the table.

He scratched his head. Caedmon appeared to be slow and methodical. Yet another man who wasn't verbose. "I'd like to look at this, without ah, well if you'd like to walk outside or something that would be fine." His face became fire truck red. He removed his glasses and wiped them with the tail of his shirt. *What's his deal?* An attorney needed to be self-assured, confident, loquacious and ready to act.

"Sure, I'll let you look over the materials." She pointed to the stack of documents he'd provided. "I'll check those out later." She closed the door and meandered through the village square. At the opposite side of the street, girls jumping rope embodied old school fun.

"May I join?"

"Yes." The girls sang a song as they swung the rope in a quick cadence, keeping the rhythm in tune with the chorus. She missed more steps than not, but they good-humoredly encouraged her.

Seattle exited a house at the end of the street with a woman on his arm. Her long licorice tinted hair flopped behind her. He said something. Angered, the woman jogged toward the education building with Seattle hot on her heels. Mac faltered and became tangled in the jump rope.

The girls laughed louder than the windchimes tinkling from the nearest house.

"Come and join us. There's room for two," she shouted to Seattle. She swung her arms, trying to get the rhythm to jump into the circle.

"Why aren't you teaching Caedmon?"

"He wanted to read the new material, alone." She reached for him. "Join me, it'll be fun."

"Seattle, jump the rope. Jump. Jump. Jump the rope." The girls sang in a sing song tone, urging him.

"Challenge accepted." His eyes glittered as he took her hand, and they entered the circle. He missed the second time the rope swooped over their heads.

She clasped his hands, and they faced each other. "Keep your eyes on me and not the rope. Concentrate on the timing. Listen, hear it? It's now at our shoulders, at the top and when it comes down toward the ground, you'll hear a swoop splat and that's your cue to jump."

Fifteen minutes later, they collapsed onto a bench. His moistened skin glimmered in the morning sun.

"You weren't concentrating." She laughed. "What had you so enraptured?"

His smile disappeared. He looked toward the hills and stood. "I've got to take a break and get a gallon of water."

She followed him into the meeting house and quietly shut the door. Caedmon sat in the corner of the room, evaluating documents.

"Are you getting much accomplished?" Seattle asked.

Slowly the boy's head lifted, and he stared. "Yes, Seattle." He didn't recoil despite Coyote's imposing wide stance.

"You aren't using Mac's services?"

"No. I wanted to review the material she brought." He glanced at them. "I'm sorry, Ms. James, I'll be ready next week. May I keep the books to review?"

"Yes. What is your focus? Injury? Criminal? Estate

planning? Land development?"

He stared at the paper in his hand. "Whatever will benefit the tribe."

"I'll return Ms. James to her home." Seattle frowned, then marched to the exit. "Ready?"

"Yes. Caedmon, is it okay for me to take those documents?"

"Yes, bring them next week, please."

"Okay. I can't wait to get on a horse again." A few yards from her cottage, she finally asked, "What happened? You went from having a smile on your face and almost laughing, back to the dismal frown and silence."

"Nothing happened. This is my usual demeanor."

"I thought I'd broken through your cold angry exterior to the warm nugget inside."

He grinned but quickly reversed the reaction into a scowl. "No warm nugget inside."

He helped her dismount from the horse, then escorted her to the door. "Do you mind if I ask a personal question?"

"Ah, I guess not." She peered at him, trying to puzzle out his thought process.

"Are you seeing someone on a regular basis?"

"Do you mean as in dating?"

He nodded.

She smiled. The man was a bizarre mix of personalities. "Not really."

"I see. Do you think I'm a geek?"

She'd done due diligence and researched Dr. Seattle Coyote. He graduated Ivy League in biochemistry and currently worked for a Fortune 500 research company. He had a penthouse in Indianapolis. Today, apparently, he must be on hiatus. She assumed his present job centered around escorting her to the tutoring session. But what else could be involved for him to stop his dedicated research? She couldn't recall the subject of his explorations, but he'd made the covers of many medical journals.

"No. When you're not growling like a coyote, you're fun. You're passably handsome." She faltered, unsure what to say.

He grimaced and mounted his horse. "I'll see you next Sunday."

"About that, I'm going to drive from now on. You're welcome to gallop here and ride with me, but I'm not into the horse-riding gig."

He shook his head. "It'll add another thirty minutes each way."

She shrugged. "I'm really good at getting to the heart of mentoring, so the travel time won't affect you."

"As you wish." He tugged Cotton Ball's reins and bolted west.

What a strange man.

****

Rob watched as Coyote rode away from Mac's house. *Interesting*. He stuffed his binoculars into the satchel and shifted his four-wheeler into drive. Several minutes later he drove through the entrance of the Native American village.

Bill, guard on duty, held up his hand. "What business do you have?"

"Hi, Bill. I need to speak to C-Eagle on an important matter."

"What matter?"

Rob put his hand on the gearshift. "It's personal."

Bill sauntered twenty feet and engaged in a conversation on his cellphone. He turned. The guard's lips disappeared inward, but he flagged Rob through the entrance.

C-Eagle stood outside the Common Building, holding a walnut handled pipe. What had been going on with Mac and the council? "Hi, Rob. What's up?"

"Morning, George." Rob glanced around. "May we speak in private?"

"Yes." The elder pivoted and lightly stepped into the building.

Rob followed, trying to decide how to approach the topic. Inside a closet-sized room, he took a seat opposite the Chief and placed his hands on his knees. "I've known you for as long as I can remember, you were my dad's best man, so you know what I have to say is the truth."

"Yes." He carefully placed the peace pipe on a table and stared.

Rob unflinchingly met his focus. "I understand McCartney James was here. Why?"

"That is our business. I'm not at liberty to share. Why is it important to you?"

Rob dug his fingers into his jeans. "I've been asked to protect her. A man, Lee Synder, attacked her several years ago, and he is due to be released from prison."

George nodded. "I get it. However, we need her assistance. She's helping us with a legal matter. What exactly do you want from us?"

Legal matter? From the research he'd done, in the last few days, she stopped practicing law. "I'm not always able to watch her, especially considering the clever woman will dig until she unearths my motive. My boss suggested her life not be disrupted by something that may or may not happen. I agree. She came to Lantern to escape the violent confusion in the east. If possible, could you provide coverage to keep an eye on her place?"

"Ah, I see. You'll have our help. I'll make sure she is guarded, at her home and while she is here." George nodded toward the door. "If you don't mind, I've another matter to attend. Don't worry, Rob, we'll take care of her."

Goal achieved; Rob stood. "Thank you."

He grinned. "Give your father my regards. I haven't seen him in a while."

"I will and the same to your family." Rob left the building and drove home; happy he had another layer of protection for Mac.

****

Mac dialed Rob's number. "Hey, you guys want to come over for dinner?"

"Sure, what time."

She glanced at the stack of green beans. "Seven, okay?"

"We'll be there." He cleared his throat. "Need us to bring anything? Marcus makes a delicious chocolate chip cookie?"

"Sounds yummy, if he has time." She disconnected, selected the music app and tapped a playlist.

She snapped the fresh beans and tossed them into the pressure cooker. An hour and five minutes until Rob and Marcus were to arrive. House clean, check. Beverages, assorted sodas and water were cooling. Banana Split Cake from Morning Bakery, check. Chicken prepped and marinating, mashed potatoes were cooked and keeping warm. All set to serve.

She placed late blooming flowers in a vase and set the bouquet in the center of the table. With the food and table ready, she showered. The doorbell rang as she finished grilling the meat

They were punctual.

"Thanks for the dinner invitation, Mac." Marcus handed her a tin box, then shoved his hands into his jean's pockets.

"Very last minute, thanks for accepting and for the treat."

"Smells delicious." Rob glanced around the kitchen.

"Chicken. I hope you guys are hungry."

"Yes." They responded in unison.

"Good, sit and we'll eat." She put oven gloves on and removed the dinner.

Their chatter, laughter, and little discussion about things that matter transformed her house into a home. One hour later she served cake, cookies, and coffee. "I want to thank you for your neighborliness."

"No prob." Marcus dug into the dessert.

"We're a community of people who help each other." Rob shoved the cake aside and lifted his coffee cup. "Hum, good coffee."

"Thanks, Brazilian."

Marcus shifted on his seat and tapped his fork to the plate.

"I have the latest version of an interactive game, box something. Interested?"

"Yes." His voice lifted an octave, as he jumped to a stand.

Rob leaned back in his chair looking relaxed and comfortable.

"I'll just show Marcus where the game is in the

office. I'll be right back."

When she returned the table had been cleared. "Thanks. You didn't have to do that."

He shrugged. "No prob."

She laughed at his perfect imitation. "Want to go outside and get some fresh air?"

He pushed away from the counter. "Sounds fine. Do you want your wine, you've barely touched it?"

"No, thanks. I'm not a fan of alcohol; however, we did get a free case of the vino." In the yard, they naturally migrated around the police tape to the wooden bench near the natural springs. Not wanting to ruin the serenity of the night, she had to know about the body. "Did the police find Liza Carpenter?"

"They have leads but haven't located her yet."

"I hope it was an accident." Mac looked at him. "Did you have fun at the dance?"

"Did you?"

"Most of the time."

"I consider last night to have been a unique and memorable experience." He chuckled. "You called Veronica the witch of Wall Street."

She tried to hide her face in her hands. "I'll never be able to look at you in the light of day again without embarrassment."

"She's just a friend, so I see her...ah...lack of niceness." He put his arm around her shoulders and brought her closer. "I think you're very refreshing." He lowered her hands, tilted her chin and lightly brushed her lips. She tasted him, tasted the coffee.

"I like you, too." She placed her hand on his neck. The memories of last night rushed in on a pulse of excitement and exhilaration. Her cellphone rang with an uplifting ringtone. "I'm sorry, I need to answer."

He nodded and went inside the house.

She answered the call. "Hi!"

"Hi, Mom. I tried a face connection but didn't get through. Do you even have service out there?"

She chuckled, knowing Cassandra was hesitant to move into the woods. "Yes, I must not have heard the call. Is everything all right?"

"Sure, just wanted to catch up."

"Good, I've company. Could I call you back in an hour?"

"Absolutely, but I want details."

"Of course. Love you. Bye."

"Later, Mom."

Marcus and Rob came from the house. "Thank you for dinner, Mac."

"You're welcome, Marcus. Anytime."

"I'll be in the truck." He loped away.

Rob's musky scent swirled around her, muddling her mind. "I was nervous about seeing you tonight."

He sighed. "I understand, you seemed discombobulated."

She laughed. "Yes, well I'm excited to have that first awkward kiss behind us."

Her cellphone gave a sharp ding, as they walked toward the truck. "You mean the peck? That's not our first real kiss, Mac."

She laughed, waved goodbye and reentered the house setting the alarm. A video connection again, but delayed, she should check the current version of her mobile device. "Hi, Xavier."

"I'm coming to visit. I can't stand to be away from you, and I'm bored, bored, bored. I'll arrive on Thursday night. Maybe we could go to a country bar on Saturday and see the yokels? I mean locals. You could hook me up with the blind date." There was a slight pause. "Are you listening?"

Mac put the cellphone on the counter, supported by a jar and towel and loaded the dishwasher. "If you're going to have an attitude about the type of people I associate with, I really don't believe you should come to southern Indiana."

"I saw your eyeroll."

"I know you're enduringly charming, witty, and you've excellent fashion taste." They'd spent many weekends going to the West End shopping for accessories. Gifted, he always selected prime merchandise.

"Of course, I do. I sense a 'but' in there." Xavier's voice held a tinge of anger.

"Throughout the years we've comforted each other after breakups and rejoiced together during the happy times." She delighted in the knowledge she had him as a support system. "I want to help you through this, but I don't know if this area of Indiana is sophisticated enough for you."

Xavier's dark mysterious eyes, short, cropped hair, and lithe body grew bigger on the screen. His inspiration helped her write the first screenplay. He provided encouragement and motivation to write story after story. "I do want to see you."

"You are so sweet, darlin'. Oops. I meant it as an endearment and with all due respect." He chuckled. "I miss you. I only have a couple of days before I must drag my sorry ass to the parents' place for Thanksgiving. Let me visit with you. We'll stay up late talking and braid each other's hair. I'll pick up your next section to be reviewed. I wouldn't mind playing doctor, while I'm there. What do you say? Yes?"

She shook her head. "Could I ever refuse you?"

"Hope not."

She smiled. "I need to call Cass. See you on Thursday. Bye."

Chapter 7

"I think you're a tad overdressed." Mac drawled. He turned, viewing his side in the nine-foot framed mirror. His features were so perfect he appeared angelic. A smoking vest with gold and navy embroidery on the front and back highlighted the blue shirt. Xavier's black jeans were enhanced by a tooled leather belt. "The big horn cowboy hat would be too much."

"You introduced me to old movies so I'm going as Doc Holiday, the best dressed of the lot. Regardless of how the TB affected his face, he looked damn good. Besides, this outfit makes my eyes shine and my skin exceptionally soft and healthy looking." He twisted his boot clad foot back and forth, admiring his dude status.

She wouldn't inflate his ego by confirming his handsomeness. "Look out western lifestyle magazine. X, I hope you find the one tonight."

Hands on his hips. "Come on. You want to say it."

"You're gorgeous. I wish you were hetero."

He chuckled. "If I were bi, we could do all that…but I'm not."

He wrapped his arm around her waist, and they walked to the car. Xavier had to slide his hat in first. "We're going to have fun."

A short drive later they arrived at their destination. "Here we are, Lasso Lou's."

The building was rustic in appearance with logs on

the outside structure. A square sign flashed in neon colors with a cowboy throwing a rope around the words Lasso Lou's Bar and Grill. A large porch ran along the front of the building, allowing party goers a place to eat and get fresh air. The windows, few and far between, were covered in gunny sack material.

"Yee Haw." His skeptical expression, in addition to the rock song blaring from a cover band generating vibrations, set the mood.

"We'll just wing it. If you're, um, comfortable then give me the sign, and I'll make an excuse to call it. Otherwise, we'll leave together. Deal?" She viewed the townspeople as loveable conservative, but what about introducing a far different type of individual. Would they be as accepting?

He glanced around as if looking for someone. "We'll leave together."

The clang of mugs being clicked together, music from the band ended, laughter and the smell of pungent onions wafted out the door as they went inside. The numerous overhead fans stirred the mix of sweat, alcohol and fried foods. She scanned the crowd but didn't see Dr. Worth. She prayed he wouldn't stand them up, making yet another injury to Xavier's already bruised ego. A loud two-fingered whistle rang through the crowed bar. She lifted on her toes and found the doctor standing at a booth toward the rear of the building.

She waved, and they wended a path toward Noah reaching him in seconds.

Noah Worth was dressed in a white cotton shirt, with pearl button snaps, and blue jeans. He had a simple black hat which didn't detract from his full head of thick blond hair. Molly told her the ladies of Lantern didn't understand why he wasn't married. When women tried to ask him for a date or fix him up with someone he always went by the idiom, can't date the patients, their friends, nor relatives. Mac thought his colleagues would be shocked to learn he accepted an invitation from an unlikely source, the newcomer.

"Hi. Found a booth and I hated to leave it to meet you at the door." He scanned the crowd, bringing his focus back to her.

"No problem. This is my friend, Xavier Montague. Xavier, this is Dr. Noah Worth." Both men examined each other and apparently found one another to their liking as smiles appeared on their faces.

Noah nodded. "Sit. Let me know what you want to drink, and I'll go to the bar."

Xavier glanced around. "I'll have a beer, light."

"I'll have a diet soda, I'm the DD tonight," she replied, then watched him saunter toward the silver metal wrapped bar. She faced Xavier. "Well, what do you think?"

"I think he's hot. Look at that tight little butt. He must work out twenty-four, seven. Maybe an hour for conversation time, and you're cleared to leave." Noah hiked his boot on the bar railing and talked with a portly older gent. "Just need to call me when you get home."

"Got it."

He sighed. "Love is in the air. Watch how he interacts with the people at the bar and the bartender. Very personable. Brainy and beautiful."

"Slow down there, easy rider."

The conversation remained light: weather, current events, and politics. The guys argued about which party would win at the next presidential election. A man with graying hair and a sharp pointed mustache approached the table. "Howdy madam. Are you with one of these hombres?"

"Yes. I'm with both." She snaked her arm through Xavier's.

"My name's Red. Red McKay. I don't see you dancing none. I say, wanna take a spin with me?"

No thanks formed on her lips, when she felt a kick on both of her chins. "Sure, I'd like to take a spin on the dance floor with you."

Thirty minutes later she'd shucked her jacket and used a paper napkin to wipe sweat from her brow. To allow her friends time to interact, she accepted a couple more requests to dance from a traveling shoes salesman and a ranch foreman. The cattleman believed in hands on dancing. She two-stepped around and away. "Gentlemen, I believe I'll call it a night."

"Great. Don't worry I'll make sure Xavier arrives safely at your house." Noah's eyes sparkled.

Xavier shoved her coat into her hands. "I'll go with you to make sure you get out unmolested."

"Thanks for walking me to the car." Settled on the driver's seat she turned on the engine and lowered the window. "Are you sure you don't want to leave with me?"

"I think he's the one. Call me, lock the house door and set the alarm, I may not be sleeping in your guest bed tonight." He presented a goofy grin.

"I'm happy for you, but keep in mind, southern Indiana is not New York. Please don't be outwardly demonstrative toward Noah, at least not in public."

"How insulting!" He laughed. "This isn't my first rodeo."

She frowned. "Actually, it is."

"No fear. I understand. Hey, will you walk Scat when you get back?" Xavier's woe-is-me expression became a cockeyed smile.

"I cannot believe you purchased a dog. A soon to be huge dog, and you brought him to my house. I didn't even know you liked dogs."

"He's a good puppy. I need to get back. Kisses." He whistled as he jogged up the stairs.

Noah opened the door and plowed into Xavier. "Are you leaving?"

She waited before backing out, in case he needed a ride.

"I thought perhaps you'd like to come to my house, so we can carry on a conversation without battling the noise." Noah hooked his thumbs in the tabs of his jeans.

"Yes. I'd like that."

Pleased with the outcome, she smiled and sang the rock song the band was playing. The joy lasted until she arrived home.

Chapter 8

"You're doing the walk of shame, so the blind date went well." Mac grouched, while making a fresh pot of coffee. "Didn't use yokel once?"

"Don't start. I've got to catch some z's before I battle wits with you." His brown eyes were road-mapped with red-lines. "Don't throw stones."

"Seriously?"

He took a step back and held his arms in surrender. "Sorry, I know that wasn't something you've ever done. Life's short, share your luscious body with that guy, your neighbor, share time with him and share your love with this man until it develops into a relationship or dies a natural death. I'm just thankful you're putting yourself out there again. You're not getting any younger."

"You're calling me old?"

"Sorry." Xavier got a bottle of water from the fridge. "Need some z's."

"By the way, look what I found when I came home last night." She turned and jerked a pair of shoes from the trash. "Very expensive Jimmy's, Xavier! They're ruined." A cool breeze blew her hair. "The back door is wide open. Where's the dog?"

"I'll replace. We need to look for him." Dark circles of exhaustion shadowed his eyes.

She rubbed her temples and chucked the pumps back in the trash. "No, I'll go, so you can order new shoes." She shoved her feet into running shoes and tied the lace twice. She didn't want to have to stop to retie them and the painfully tight knots helped divert some of her anger. "Scat will return with you to the city. I don't have time for a dog. Understand?"

He straightened and gave her a salute. "Aye! Aye!"

She jerked an athletic jacket off the hook near the back door and went in search of a curious shoe-eating wolfdog. The grass crunched under her feet where the sun had yet to melt the frost, leaving a faint path of pawprints. He'd taken a straight course across the meadow.

What seemed like miles later she was ready to abandon the chase. His path had dissipated, allowing her to guess the direction. Her gaze followed the fence outlining her property. A red-orange pick-up truck glistened in the rays. Huddled over a post a man wrapped wire with a large pair of pliers. His strong back was covered by duck-cloth type material. A black hat shielded his features. Harmless? She took a deep breath and reminded herself she wasn't in the east.

She ran to his side. "Excuse me, sir. I'm looking for a puppy. Have you seen a little gray and white escapee?"

"Do you mean this dog, Mac?" Rob straightened and stood. Her heart stopped beating. She put her hands to her chest in case the organ didn't restart.

"Are you okay? You look pale."

"Yes. Fine. Just worried." Her breath came out in wisp of air. *Act normal.* She shoved her hands into her pockets and turned toward Scat.

"I didn't know you had a dog." Scat had a piece of twine tied from his dog collar to the fence post. He snored and his legs moved back and forth as if he chased a rabbit or squirrel.

"I don't. It belongs to a friend. His name is Scat."

"Your friend or the dog?"

"The dog's name is Scat."

"Like Scat Cat?"

"No, more like Scat the jazz music, do dop do to, da-ditty-do. My friend has an unusual sense of humor." She lowered onto her hunches and rubbed the gray and white underbelly of Scat. As she anticipated he rolled over. She stood again. Rob leaned against the fence post. He removed his hat, then replaced it.

Mac answered his unstated question. "Xavier, my friend, was dating a musician at the time he purchased the dodger. A British musician, nonetheless, who enjoyed jazz music. Especially scatting. They're no longer dating; however, Scat has been embossed in the young shoe-eaters furry head and sometimes responds to that name."

"It appears to be a mixture of wolf and some fue fue dog, perhaps a poodle. Judging by the paws, he's going to be big. Not too late to change the name."

"Great minds think alike. I mentioned the name change idea to Xavier, and he promptly brought up a video on his phone and cast it to the TV. The theme from a kid's show came on and Scat ran over and plopped his fuzzy K-9 butt in front of the television. Xavier selected a chapter, and a bright furry puppet came onto the screen singing a nonsense song." Heat rose to her face.

He lifted his eyebrows.

"Super Monkey, you're the one, I'll make you a raft of fun, Super Monkey I'm awfully fond of …Mo-scoop, tada-ditty-mo-mo-scoop. Scat was in doggy paradise." She took a deep breath. "By your expression I've shared way too much."

Rob ambled to the truck bed. He reached into the back, opened a cooler, and drew out a couple of bottles of water. "Here. You've had quite a walk."

"Yes, friend left the door open. He's leaving on Sunday. Scat obeys one command; sit but only for that one song." She drizzled water into her mouth. *Shut up, no wonder why he hasn't called you to ask you on a date.* She tucked the bottle under her arm and untied the twine at the fence. "Thank you for keeping him here and for the water."

She took a second long cooling drink, resisting the urge to ask why he hadn't called. They had a lovely time at the vineyard, well certainly a memorable time. Okay, she did embarrass herself the night of the barn dance; however, the following night at dinner all was well. Yet, no phone call. She turned to go. "I'll let you get back to work. Have a nice weekend."

"Have you heard the history of Lantern?" He lifted his water bottle and pointed it toward the town. "I saw the numerous books in your living room, so I know you are keenly interested in history, facts, and travel."

She stopped and turned. "No. I haven't heard the story. I assume you're going to tell me?"

The dimple flashed briefly. "I'd love to tell you. Climb in and I'll show you Star Point." He walked to the passenger side, reached through the open window and unlatched the door from the inside. "Come on Mac, you're a curious one."

She heaved a sigh and lifted the puppy into the truck cab, then climbed onto the seat and searched for a seatbelt.

"There aren't any, a hand strap is above if you need

it." He grinned.

"You appear to enjoy vintage trucks. Is this color red or is it all rust?"

"Mostly rust. Hang on." They drove on a path created from repeated use, with the truck springs squeaking upon dipping into each pothole. "Lewis and Clark on their famous expedition west traveled this area summer of 1803. They docked their 17-meter-long keelboat on the Ohio River and ultimately stopped in Clarksville, Indiana. While traversing the Ohio, the group came upon a bog." He took a swig of water.

"Lee Floyd was the pilot. Craggy rocks make the Falls of Ohio difficult to navigate. The channel is crooked and the water furious and swift. It takes a great deal of dexterity to pilot through the four miles."

She moved to the center of the seat, allowing Scat to lean his head out the window. His tongue flopped about in the wind and carried drool to the rear.

"Lee's cousin, Sam M. Floyd was assisting in extracting the boat captained by Webster Z. Gates, Lieutenant for the United States Army, which was caught in a bog when a water moccasin, a snake, bit his lower leg. Hours later Floyd's temperature was extremely elevated. They needed medical help." He stopped the truck and shut down the engine. "Here we are. Do you want to get out and walk?"

"Sure. This is Star Point? I don't see anything resembling a river, which would produce such great rapids that a pilot was needed."

"Yes, Star Point. Come on, I'll show you." The door released a high-pitched squeak as he stepped outside. Scat jumped over her and onto the mossy ground. Rob assisted her from the truck, took her hand into his and led her toward the cliff. The dog trailed behind, sniffing and exploring. The closer they got to the edge of the land the louder the cascading water could be heard. Moist dank brine permeated the air.

Rob sat on a grassy area and held out his hand. She retrieved Scat's tether and sat beside the storyteller. "Is there more?"

"Of course. A pitch-black night seemed to come on suddenly, which prevented them from clearly spotting land. The chill in the air created an atmosphere of concern for the injured man. Fortunately, as they were careening along the rapids they came to a turning point where a piece of land extended out into the water, and they saw a light. A beacon." He softened his voice, and she was sure it was for effect.

"A lighthouse?"

"Kind of. They successfully pulled their vessels onto land. Quickly anchoring the keel boats, they climbed the embankment with the intent to make camp. At the top they saw a beautiful Native American. Her name was Water Star and a member of the Miama tribe. The light was a carved pumpkin with a candle inside. A side note, the natives preserve bits of the fruit to make a type of dessert jerky. Clever resourceful people."

"A lantern." Next year she'd plant a garden with pumpkins. *Concentrate, he's setting up a scene.* She placed a leg under the other.

"Water Star had a white tutor, so she had excellent English. She offered her assistance and took them back to her campsite where Floyd was further treated for his snakebite."

"And that is why the commissioners of Floyd County, Indiana, decided to name the town Lantern?"

Charmed by the story, she imagined Founder's Day would be in the fall. She must have been moving when the special day was commemorated.

"No. It continues. Do you want to hear the ending?"

"Oops, sorry. I guess I like to draw conclusions. Go ahead." She unfolded her legs and finger-combed Scat's fine fur.

"There's nothing more beautiful than a Miama woman in her prime. The young nubile Water Star offered to care for Sam Floyd. Sam, being a man with common sense, celebrated. According to his journal, her honey brown firm skin was incredible to touch. Her long black braided hair brushed against his chest. Her sweetheart-shaped face highlighted dark chestnut eyes." Rob cleared his throat. He looked embarrassed. She bit her lip, resisting the urge to giggle.

"Sam wrote her eyes shone brightly like the stars in a night sky, enchanting him. He fell hopelessly in love."

"And she fell hopelessly in love with him, and they named the town after the lantern which brought them together." She released a long breath and smiled.

He tugged her closer to his side and moved his lips close to her ear. "No, impatient woman, would you rather have an ending of your choice?" Rob's voice held hints of humor.

"Sorry. I promise not to interrupt again."

"Water Star did fall in the love with the white man, which created problems within her tribe. Samuel tried to bargain with the chief to make her his wife, but she'd been promised to Little Bear. The day before the expedition was due to leave Sam arranged to meet Water Star at the point, which is now called Star Point. He planned to sneak her into the keelboat. While on water, the captain of the ship, Clark, could marry them."

Scat settled between them. Rob scratched the pup's back. "Little Bear overheard the conversation and held her captive. When Water Star didn't show up at the rendezvous point Samuel believed she'd changed her mind. At the break of dawn, they were preparing to shove off the landing when Water Star finally broke through her binds. Running to the point, she frantically waved. One of the pirogue canoes, closer to the shore, turned to go back and retrieve her. As her father and Little Bear approached, she knew she had one chance to be with the man she loved."

"Oh no." Mac wrapped the dog's rope around her hand.

"She jumped from the highest peak and swam toward the boat. Water Star was named because of her strength as a swimmer. However, the current was extreme that day and the force pulled her under. Her leg caught in a snag. Sam jumped into the water. He found her, floating in the murky depths of the Ohio River. He didn't go with Lewis & Clark's Corps of Discovery mission but stayed and developed the town of Lantern. Sam Floyd forever mourned his lost love, Water Star."

"I take it back. I'd rather have the ending of my choice."

He used the edge of his shirtsleeve to wipe away her tears.

"Mac, do all of your stories have happy endings?"

What? Like she didn't know something bad could happen in life. There was a three-inch file in the NYPD with real life written all over it. "Oh course. Who wants to see a movie about true life stories where the bad guy wins, or star-crossed lovers never get together? People who see my movies expect a rousing story with some intrigue. Ultimately, they want to know the couple ends up together and happily-ever-after could be their future."

"So, you're not a realist?"

"I am, but I'm more of a romantic. I believe in destiny and karma. Don't you?" She leaned into his neck and inhaled his scent, a mixture of sun, sweat, and woodsy cologne.

"I believe a man or woman can change his or her destiny by making choices. The fork in the road. Good versus evil. Karma." He'd made mistakes in the past and hesitated to approach the topic of them as a couple who dated.

"Yes. We all make choices." She stood and brushed her pants. Scat jumped to a stand and circled, getting the rope caught on a thin willow tree.

He pointed toward the hound. "I'll take you home."

"Oh, Scat. You're so mischievous. What will I do with you?" She guided the dog back around the tree.

A short quiet drive to her house, Rob parked and turned toward her. With the dog in her arms, she catapulted from the truck. She rushed inside and released Scat from his bondage. He drank from his water bowl, then plopped onto the floor. She ignored Xavier's arched brow and opened the freezer door.

"How did it go?" He finger-combed his hair and yawned loudly.

"Found him a few miles away. You should be careful with a puppy. It's like a baby. Takes time and care." She drew a baker's box from the freezer and carried it to the kitchen counter.

Xavier opened the refrigerator, searched the contents and removed a bottle of juice.

"What are you guys going to do tonight? I'll leave you the code if you want to come here after a date?" Knife poised over the chocolate cake; she smiled at him. "I'm meeting a friend."

"No, you're not." His focus remained on the knife.

"No, I'm not what?" She slid the blade into the cake.

"You left your phone, and a guy named Luke called. Canceling, with regrets. He sounded old. Who is he?"

"Rob's father. We met at the barn dance. I like him, he's friendly." Chocolate was a sedative for bad news, even at seven A.M.

"Ah, moonshine Luke. He's friendly and related to the guy you want to bang?"

Mac shot him a glare. "It never hurts to get to know people who live in your community. You go have a ball for both of us."

"Ha. Pun intended." Xavier headed toward the guest bedroom. "Watch the waist."

"Since it takes you hours to get ready, you might start now." Jealousy would be her bedfellow tonight. She pressed Molly's contact. "Hi, on Wednesday your brother-in-law arrives, right?"

"Right." Her voice was hesitant.

"I'm looking to date, so we'll do an intro with that in mind." Firm and decisive she closed the lid on the cake box without removing the slice.

"What about Rob? I thought you wanted to fly solo with the big guy?"

"I don't understand him. He acted interested in pursuing a relationship and then a moment later he backs away. So, I'm moving on."

"What about your heart? Is it moving on too?"

"You always go for the inner core. The heart's just

a muscle and like any other muscle it can be stretched. Currently, it's maxed out with lingering fuzzy warm thoughts of Rob, but it can be shrunk again as well. Let me know what to bring on Thursday." She tried to interject an upbeat tone.

"Terrific. A beverage or dessert, your choice." Excitement riddled through her voice. "You're going to like Nick."

"Thank you." She glanced out the kitchen window. A strange man leaned over the police tape at the springs. She grabbed her taser and ran into the yard. "May I help you?"

He jerked upright; a sprinkle of water fell from a test tube. "Hi. Ms. James?"

"Yes." She clutched the taser at her side.

He twisted the lid on the container and removed his cap. "I'm Sam Goodnight. Rob Barringer asked me to evaluate the water in your springs."

The conservation officer. Every muscle in her body relaxed. "Thank you. I appreciate your help. Will the water be contaminated due to Carpenter's accident?"

He cocked his head and walked closer. "We'll know more after I get the results from the tests." Sam glanced at the house. "You know he was murdered."

"No, I didn't know that." A light came on in the bathroom. Through the window she could clearly see Xavier's silhouette. She had to get better curtains. "Do I need to leave the tape in place?"

"It's been several weeks, they've probably gotten all of the evidence they needed, so take it down." Sam extended his hand. "It's nice to meet you, Ms. James."

She shook his hand. "Nice to meet you too, Mr. Goodnight."

Chapter 9

As far as first impressions go, Nick Black didn't resemble his brother physically or in personality. He had thick ebony hair, a mustache over a thin upper lip and tawny eyes. She liked her date to be taller than her, and he was eye level. The compensation was that he had a nice shape, and his manners were impeccable.

During Thanksgiving dinner, he told humorous stories about their childhood. A successful architect, he'd encountered a few unusual clients in Kentucky. Characters so well defined she had an intense desire to go directly home and detail them into her current screenplay.

"Are you ready to call it a night?" After dinner they played a popular card game until the pairing of men finally won.

"Yes, I'm very tired." She covered a yawn with her hand.

"Don't forget tomorrow morning we work off the turkey by playing flag football in Centennial Park. It's a tradition," Matt excitedly exclaimed.

Molly rolled her eyes. "Matt relives his days of shining glory as a high school star quarterback on this one day each year. The Thanksgiving football game is serious business."

Nick insisted on chauffeuring by following her home and walking her to the door. "Aren't you going to invite me in for a drink?" He had a whine in his voice. One of his hands rested on her shoulder, then his thick fingers crept up her neck.

She shivered. "It's late and tomorrow will be such an early start." She wasn't sure if she liked him or not. He was pleasant to be around and handsome in a boy-next-door way. However, his kiss was wet, and the whine was difficult to get past. Damn Rob for creating a tempest.

"One drink and a little conversation." He edged closer, backing her into the doorframe. "I leave in two days, so we've a limited time together. This trip anyway."

"Guess not. I'm sorry, but I'm tired." Her eye scan unlocked the door. "Thank you." She turned on all the lights. Scat slowly rose from his pet pillow to greet her. What an oxymoron; scatting was a quick tune, while the dog was a slow-moving unenthusiastic canine. She rubbed his head. "Hi fella! Miss me?"

Scat gave a half-hearted woof, then growled at the stranger entering his territory.

"He doesn't like me." Nick stepped back. "But you do, right?"

"You're a nice guy, but I'm interested in someone else."

"Give me a name, maybe I can share some information which will change the playing field." He apparently didn't like to lose.

"I'm sorry, I'm sure you'll find the perfect woman, it's not me." She pushed him further onto the porch. "I'll see you tomorrow at the game." She set the alarm and threw herself onto the couch.

****

Late for the football game, Rob backed into a tight end spot. Nick Black put his right hand on Mac's rear. Rob tightened his grip on the steering wheel.

"Dad, are we going to join them?" Marcus, impatient, drew the strings on his sweatshirt together.

"Sure, let's show them what the Barringer men can do with a football." Rob carried a cooler full of water, protein drink and juice. Marcus had extra blankets. They approached the group. His son was all smiles. Rob waited at the sidelines, while Marcus joined his friends.

The sun created blind spots on the playing field. Brisk coldness, so cold it froze the hairs lining his nose, wouldn't detract the team's desire to win. The pigskin went high and long in the air. With a downward spiral, it came directly in front of her. Her eyes widened. She caught the orb and sought an opportunity to cast the sphere off to the nearest teammate, then ran maneuvering in and out of the holes in the defense line. A break occurred. Her expression of excitement made his gut clinch. Nick hovered at the twenty fifth yard line. She glanced to the left and quickly to the right then hurled the ball to her closest co-player. At the same time Matt grabbed her from behind, and she went down. Rob knew from prior experience the freshly cut, late autumn, grass tasted earthy, and grinned as she spat. *She is adorable.*

Matt, panting, extended his huge southpaw to Mac. "Are you okay?"

"Yes, I just need a minute." She rolled over and touched her cheek. A bit of grass fell off.

"You're going to have a nice blue, purple and red bruise tomorrow."

Timothy Black danced around, as any nine-year-old can do after a day of play. "To be a Titan you need to take the fall, and you did. You're tough for an old girl." His blue-on-blue jersey was two sizes too big and flapped as fast as his mouth. Nick ran forward and reached down. She took hold of Matt's hand. "Did we get the goal?"

"Yes, we did thanks to you and Nick," Molly answered and elbowed Mac, then nodded toward them.

"Great timing you guys, we can use you on our team." Matt nodded to Rob.

"What's the score?" He couldn't take his glace from her. Nick's arm, seemingly attached to Mac's waist, hadn't moved. Rob didn't consider himself the jealous type, but he didn't see a world where someone else was touching her.

She bent to retie her shoe and edged away.

"Hey, Rob." Nick's focus switched from Mac to him. "You're welcome to join us, although I don't think any pro football player could help Matt's team at this point."

"Rah-Rah-Rah, you can boast because you're up by one goal, but we'll catch up." Matt punched Rob's arm.

Molly failed to calm Timothy. The kid might have a hyperactive disorder.

"If we've two-star quarterbacks, even if one is old, they should separate which makes the number uneven on Mom's team," David declared.

"I need to go." Mac glanced at Marcus. "I'll bow out while my name is still in fame for the assist of the last touchdown. Could one of you take my place?"

Nick grabbed her hand. "Don't go. We'll substitute people in and out."

"I really need to get to the rewrites." She freed her hand. "Molly and Matt, I had a lovely time. Thank you for inviting me."

"I need to get my hat out of the car. I'll be right back. There are drinks in the cooler." Nick followed Mac, keeping on her heels

She placed her fingers on the door latch, and the sensor quickly clicked. Pepper spray in hand, she turned.

"Whoa." Nick jumped.

"Am I interrupting?"

"Rob." Relief flooded her voice. Maybe there wasn't anything developing between them.

"Is there something I can help you with?" Nick's mouth tightened into a straight line.

"Yes. Will you excuse us?" Rob extended a hand.

"No." Nick grabbed her arm and tugged. "I want to see you. Can I come by later?"

"No. I've deadlines to meet. No free time. Please enjoy the rest of your visit."

"Mac," he begged.

"The lady wants you to leave, Nick, and apparently not bother her again."

"None of your business, Barringer," he spewed.

"Yes, it is. We're together," Rob snapped. Mac's eyes widened.

"Is this true? Is this the guy you mentioned last night?"

"Nick, I've enjoyed getting to know you, as a friend, but I need to talk with Rob."

Nick marched toward the group, hovering near the coolers.

"Last night?" Rob softly asked.

"We had a date." She pointed toward Molly. "The four of us."

"And?" He moved his focus along her body to the

ground and back.

"I don't sleep around. I thought you and I had a connection; an affinity I haven't found for many years. By the implication you just made, I must be wrong. Goodbye, Rob." Her eyes shot hot anger.

"Just now, he was handsy. You've accused, tried and sentenced me without ever listening to my thoughts."

She got into the car, snapped the seatbelt in place and drove away.

Torn between the desire or need to develop a relationship with Mac or simply extend an olive branch of friendship ripped through him. The night of the dance he experienced Veronica's foul mouth and bad-tempered side. She tried the sad, you-don't-love-me-anymore act, then went polar and called him vulgar names, words he wouldn't have expected. He ended the friendship and vowed to avoid women, except keeping his emotional distance from Mac was becoming virtually impossible.

Chapter 10

Lee Snyder watched and waited, something in which he exceled. Enjoyment rippled through him. He reveled in her unfolding story, planning to patiently observe her from afar. Although the police database listed him as violent, he was simply a man who loved to stand and gaze upon the beauty of this graceful seductive woman.

Restricted from writing letters to Mac, he did his jail time. Once paroled, he discovered she'd changed locations. Her daughter had also changed addresses, so he couldn't get information about her or additional facts regarding his dream girl. Despite her secrecy, he'd found her.

Clever girl, the jokes on you MK, I followed the fag to your house. He laughed. *I'll insist you let me into your life.* Yes, he would have her. No one would see her but him. She'd be preserved, forever.

He lifted the binoculars and gazed at her when she entered the bathroom. The thin curtains provided a haze over her body, amping his desire and possessive need. A male opera singer resonated about love and the absence of love. He didn't know anything about opera, but since he shared so much with MK, he'd done his research and tolerated her odd taste.

With each stroke of her hand swiping the cloth along her body, he yanked his manhood. *How wonderful that cleanliness is close to godliness.* MK's ablution was, for him, a secret addiction consuming his soul. The baritone's crescendo was his crescendo as well. Lee emptied on the hot springs rock wall.

He refastened his trousers. A gray-haired tall, lithe, man arrived. She kissed the old guy on the cheek. The gent entered the house. He crushed his cigarette with his work boot, digging into the moist ground. Another day or two and he'd make her aware of his skills, then take possession.

****

Mac released the alarm and pulled open the door, letting in the fresh fall scents of leaves and mums, apparently wild mums because she hadn't been in the garden for weeks.

"Am I too early?" Luke Barringer sauntered bow-legged into the cottage.

"No, I'm running late. I didn't want to break the rhythm. I usually give myself time for a last-minute clothing change, which means now I need to make the choice stick." She kissed his deeply lined cheek. He reminded her of her father, who also smelled of wintergreen. The remembrance brought a tear to her eye and a desire to cling to him and never let go. "Make yourself at home."

"No hurry, do you have coffee?" He removed the coat to reveal a black sweater and weathered ebony jeans.

"Sure. Nothing fresh in the pot, but here's a single coffee maker," she opened a cupboard, "and a variety of coffee pods."

Mac tugged on a tan cashmere sweater for warmth, dark brown wool slacks, a chocolate and black Houndstooth jacket and slipped on taupe leather half-boots. She walked into the great room to find Luke sipping coffee and reading her screenplay. The man lacked a moral compass.

He glanced up and smiled. "It's funny, Mac. I like the couple. They continue to cross paths, argue, touch on the edge of love and retreat. I think I know who you're modeling them after."

She laughed, removed a pair of warm gloves from the coat closet and placed them in her bag. "Think so?"

He flipped through the pages. "May I take this," he held the manuscript, "and return it tomorrow when I pick you up for the award ceremony?"

She smiled. "Sure, it'll give me a much-needed break from writing tonight."

"You're creative."

Heat rushed to her cheeks. "Well, um, I guess we should go. Oops, I need to take Scat outside. Do you want to go with?" She got the leash off the coat rack and walked toward the dog.

He chuckled and bent to pet the puppy. "Come along, scalawag?"

"He is a scamp. Yesterday my clothes, from the laundry basket, were strewn everywhere. Don't get me started on the shoes."

"Puppies are like children, into everything. On Clark Street, there's a guy who's excellent in shoe repair. His name is Barry Johnson. Tell him I sent you."

"Thanks, Luke. I said the same thing to the owner, who mysteriously left the shoe-eater in my care." She hesitated. "Have you heard anything about the man, Carpenter, who was found in the hot springs?" Mac released the button on the leash, allowing Scat to run to the nearest bush.

"Yes. Rumor has it the Mrs. had an affair. She did her husband in and now she can't be found."

Scat ran between her legs. "Do you know who the other party is?"

"Do you mean the other man? No." His lips formed a tight line, and his eyes narrowed into slits.

"Wow, that's a reaction. We don't need to talk about the Carpenters." Scat did his business, and she put him in the house. Bag in hand, she reset the security and settled onto the passenger seat and smiled at Luke. "Give me some idea about the screenplay. What's your take on what should happen next?"

"Um, not sure. I'll finish reading the section first."

Moments later they arrived at the high school. The football stadium was packed. They walked along the concrete pathway. "Molly Black is saving us a seat, so we need to look for her and Matt."

"Over here, Mac." Molly waved furiously.

****

Rob's heart skipped a beat as Luke escorted Mac along the metal bleachers. She'd mentioned a Luke at the barn dance. His unlucky streak continued as moonshine Luke was his father.

"Rob, your father's dating your obnoxious neighbor." Veronica stood in the row in front of him.

"None of your business."

Veronica sneered and wiggled her way to the end of the row. Sam Goodnight kissed her cheek and grinned.

The players ran off the field at half-time, Rob rose and clapped to cheer the team, glowing with pride for his son. He moved to an empty seat beside her. "Hi, Mac."

"Hi, Rob. Awesome first half. David's toss to

number 32 was the turning point. They're sure to have a victory." She glanced at him and then toward the right.

"Steaming hot beverage with a little cream for my lady." Luke held an insulated cup.

"Thanks, Luke, exactly what I needed. Hmmm, decadent coffee."

Rob's stomach clenched as she breathed in deeply, exactly as she'd done to his neck.

"Luke." Rob nodded.

"Great game. Marcus's doing well." Luke stated with a broad smile that collapsed his deep lines into grooves.

"Yes, he's having a good season. Mac, did your friend and his dog return to New York?" His eyes were level with her delicious pink-reddish tinted mouth.

She grinned. "My friend returned and left Scat. I've a house guest who seriously needs obedience training."

"I'll help you train him, if you like." He magnanimously offered, trying to get back into her good graces.

"What a nice idea. Rob's a professional with animal behavior. His horse training skills are renown throughout several states. You should accept his offer," Luke insisted.

He suspected Luke had an ulterior motive, probably something downright devious. Mac bounced a glance between them.

"If you've the free time, Rob, I'll be more than happy to accept your offer." Her grin was lopsided. "I'm running out of footwear."

"How does tomorrow sound?"

"Great any time before four in the afternoon, I've a date." She smiled affectionately at Luke.

He grinned. "She does, with me. We're going to the Lantern Historical Society's benefit."

"Are you two becoming an item?" What the hell; he shouldn't give a damn.

"Would it bother you if we did?" Luke's accusatory expression told him everything he needed to know about the relationship, platonic. Oh course, he'd misjudged before, so the assumption could be misleading.

"No. You can do what you want. You always do. Won't bother me a bit." He didn't keep the resentment out of his tone.

"Rob." A shout, from a cluster of his rowdy guys, caught his attention.

"Mac, I'll be over in the early afternoon." Rob walked toward his friends gathered around the refreshment booth.

Chapter 11

"Sorry I'm late. I've had an inconceivably chaotic day. My stud busted the fence to mate with the females in heat. Fight broke out between two bulls. I finally got them separated, I still had the fence to fix, and you don't need to hear all of this." Rob removed his hat and ran his hand through his hair.

"Hey, no problem; next time just call to cancel. You didn't have to make a trip over here." Mac held Scat's leash tight. For some bizarre reason he wanted to jump on Rob. He hadn't exhibited this behavior before, was the best yet to come?

"Actually, I want to be here. I know your timeline ends at four. However, the first several days the training should be kept short. Puppies tire easy and lose interest. You still want to begin?" He petted Scat. The dog whimpered from deep in his throat, laid on Rob's boots, then rolled to his back. Tongue hanging out, his tail beat the floor.

"Traitor," she whispered. "Ok, I'll get a couple of treats and his squeaky ball." She handed the leash to Rob and removed a toy from the dog basket. "Do you think two treats will be enough?"

"Should be." They walked into the yard. Scat stopped to do his business. Praise by Rob brought about another round of sharp tail twitching. Indeed, the man had a way with animals.

"Try to hold a training session twice a day for about fifteen minutes. Work in a private environment, then move to the public area. Find out what your dog likes, apparently the ball and bones or treats, and reward him. Try to break off bits of the treat before you begin training, because the broken pieces fall to the ground. The dog picks up the scent and is distracted, which is frustrating for both of you. How is he handling the little things, like the noise of a vacuum cleaner, umbrella, grooming, etc.?"

"Fine. Most of this was ingrained before he landed in my lap. He seems to be adjusting to country noises. The beast doesn't mind having his teeth brushed. I struggle to get the brush from between his jaws."

"Lucky for you. If he appears to be frightened, you'll want to soothe or calm him. It's normal for him to show signs of uneasiness when coming face-to-face with something new. Let him explore, within reason, to learn."

For the next fifteen minutes, they trained Scat. He walked, sat, rolled over, which wasn't a command, he simply liked to scratch his back on any spot of dirt. The canine reacted enthusiastically to Rob's calm, controlled voice. A level of trust began to form between all three of them.

"Oh my gosh! The time. I've got to run." She called Scat. He chose that moment to exhibit his lying down and rolling skill.

Rob chuckled. "Go ahead, I'll play ball with him for a few minutes, then put him in the house."

"Thanks, Rob. I didn't know how I'd calm his excitement."

****

"That's what neighbors and friends do for each other, Mac." A light winked in a nearby foliage overgrowth. Rob waved, knowing a native was watching. He tossed the ball. Scat grabbed hold of the rubber orb and shook his head back and forth. He loved a challenge, and both the dog and Mac were proving to be a pleasure to be around.

Scat dropped the ball in front of him. Rob heaved the globe. Carried by the brisk fall wind the orb fell into the trees. Scat ran with a puppy gait, rear out to the side and both back legs hopping. The woods held a lot of unusual scents, and an un-tethered dog could be gone for hours. He got the leash and entered the group of conifers nearest the house. Scat sniffed fast and furious around the base of a tree. A squirrel chattered, with his gray tail flipping back and forth, protecting his home from the furry invader.

"Scat. Sit."

Scat plopped his derrière onto the ground but continued to breathe like a steam engine. He snapped the clasp of the leash on the dog collar. Cigarette butts littered the ground, recently smoked. A few had been smashed into the ground; the rest were full and dry. As far as he could tell, Mac jogged regularly, which wasn't a sign of a smoker. Rob turned 360 degrees. The sight of Mac, in the bathroom, standing in front of the mirror in only a skimpy towel took his breath away. With quick swipes of a small brush, she dusted her face and with each movement his heart raced. He knew who would be smoking outside her bathroom window. He used a leaf to pick up one of the butts and carried it to his truck. He removed a plastic collection sample bag used for cattle's dung and placed the evidence inside.

****

They arrived early at the banquet. Luke, as master of ceremonies, discussed the agenda with another member of the Society. Name cards were at each table, and she quickly found her seat. Rob, Marcus, and Lindsay also had place markers. Mac sat alone at the table, waiting. A gentle touch on her shoulder brought her around.

"Sorry, I'm late." Rob took the name place card for Lindsay and exchanged it with his. He sat and signaled a server. "Coffee, please. Mac?"

"No, I'm good. Thank you. Why didn't you mention you were coming?"

"Ladies and gentlemen, I welcome you to the one hundred and fifth ceremony dedicated to showering appreciation on our community members." The microphone squealed, followed by clinking and clanking. Lucas nervously chuckled.

Their closeness stirred her hyper-sensitivity as her nostrils pulled in each scent, the man, the cologne, the coffee. His finger thumped a fast tune on the tabletop. He moved his legs, which bumped the table. He had a slight bit of graying at his temples and crinkles around his eyes from the sun, age and oh so desirable laughter. "Where's Veronica?"

"She isn't coming. We aren't seeing each other." Their glances connected.

"Oh." A quick and immense infusion of hope flooded the main artery of her heart. There may be a chance. The fluttering in her stomach intensified. Don't forget he insinuated you slept with Nick. She took a deep breath and exhaled.

"Sorry we're late, Dad. Have we missed very much?

Hi, Mac, you look fabulous." Marcus settled on the seat across from her. Lindsay slid onto the chair beside him.

"Yes, you missed the entire opening dialogue, disrespectful to your grandfather. You may've been able to contemplate some of his words of wisdom." Rob's voice held a faint trace of humor.

"Who do you think wrote the opening dialogue for him? Did you like the joke involving the ranch hand, sheep, and a maiden?" Marcus glanced between her and Rob.

Her face flooded with heat. Rob frowned, then focused on rearranging his silverware.

"I see. Then you didn't listen to the speech or my witty joke. What have you two been doing?" A wide smile replaced the youngster's look of decorum.

"Why are you late?"

"Traffic." Marcus lifted his water glass; condensation clouded the sides.

Rob lifted an eyebrow. "One traffic light in the city, how could traffic be a delay?"

Change the subject. She glanced into the girl's dark brown eyes, matching her perfectly angled ombre hairstyle. "Lindsay, what university are you going to next year and what do you want to study?"

The teen's pageant smile broke the tension. "I plan to go to the University of New York State. If I'm granted entrance, I intend to study acting. I'm looking for an internship for this summer. I'll have a better chance of getting admitted if I had some actual experience."

Marcus scrutinized Lindsay. "I told you not to ask. I'm glad we're over."

Mac sent him a questioning look. The kid shrugged his shoulders.

"I could probably help you get an internship for the summer, if you don't mind being an assistant, really a person who fetches items for the assistant."

"Oh, you'd help me, Ms. James?" She blinked, making her two-inch lashes rest on her cheeks.

"I'm always willing to support young entrepreneurs of our country. Could you spend the summer in the east?"

"Yes, I could. Thank you." She hesitated and grimaced. "You'll help me even if I'm not Marcus's girlfriend?"

"Lindsay, we agreed," Marcus said. Lindsay studied her salad. "We were late tonight, because we decided to split up."

It must be in the air. "Lindsay, if your parents approve, I'll make some calls and write a letter of introduction."

"Thank you, Ms. James, I'll have them call you."

"Since you got what you came for, I'll take you home." Marcus stood. He'd inherited the Barringer thunderous facial expression.

"Why don't you and Lindsay stay for the rest of the banquet?" Rob made the request sound more like a command.

"No, thank you Mr. Barringer, I'd rather go home. Thank you, Ms. James. I'll drop off a resume tomorrow."

Luke arrived at the table. "Where are you going? They are starting to serve the main course."

"Sorry, Grandfather, Lindsay isn't feeling well. I'm going to take her home. See you later. Dad. Mac." Marcus followed her from the room.

"What was that all about?" He sat beside Mac and dug into his salad.

"They aren't going to date each other any longer." Rob moved his empty water glass and took hold of Marcus'.

"Good, never cared for her anyway. She seemed to be a little self-centered." He wiggled his fingers at the waiter. "Coffee, please."

"She's artistic." Mac felt sorry for the couple. The relationship road wasn't always smooth and straight.

"Where's the witc…um, Veronica this evening?" He took a roll from the center breadbasket, then glanced at Rob. "Oh, not a good night for the Barringer men, eh?"

"Luke." His narrowed eyed stare emphasized his grumble.

"What? No break-up in our future. We're not dating, just hanging out. Right, Mac?" He lifted his cup.

"Right, Luke. We're buddies, sharing time and space." She lifted her water glass and clicked it against his cup.

"Then you won't mind if I drive her home tonight?" Rob asked.

"Damn straight I do. A gentleman who escorts a lady returns her to her residence." He glanced between them, making heat rush to her face.

The Widow Haven, in a flurry of silk and strong floral perfume, placed her hand on Luke's shoulder, drawing his attention. A very skilled surgeon must have rolled back time on the woman's face. "Luke. Fun opening commentary. I especially liked the joke, not offensive at all."

"Why, thank you, Madeline. There's an alternate I considered. Want to hear the ripper?" The older couple continued their nonstop squabbling.

"I need to talk to you in private. May I see you

later?" Rob whispered.

An entire battalion of winged insects fluttered around in her stomach. She ignored any negative thoughts and glanced into his sky blues. "Yes, I'll be home directly after the event."

****

Rob softly knocked on Mac's recently painted blue door. Furniture legs squeaked against hardwood floors, adding cadence to the elevator music she had playing. A few seconds later the door opened. "Hi."

She grinned. "Hi, yourself."

Scat rose from his bed, yawned, then ambled toward him. Rob stroked the odd-looking dog's rough fur. Mac had changed into tight-fitting black athletic pants and a matching t-shirt. He resisted the urge to stroke her clenched jaw. Instead, he sat on the dark gray sofa. "Let's talk."

Her brilliant white teeth pulled her full upper lip down, upon release it flipped back red and fuller. She moseyed over and dropped heavily on the other end of the couch. Scat plopped directly on top of his boots.

He took one of Mac's hands into his. "I'm sorry. I would like to say what you said at the football game was wrong; however, you were right I did imply that you slept with Nick. In the back of my mind I thought, maybe, just maybe you were playing the field."

Mac tried to break the connection. He tightened the grip. "No, please, listen. I don't know you. I want to know you. I felt a connection, too." A whoosh of air flowed from his mouth, giving him a sense of ease. "Due to my past relationship mistakes I've been, unsuccessfully, denying the attraction."

She blinked. "Do you want to talk about the

113

mistakes?" Pink cheeked, she tucked a piece of hair behind an ear.

"Maybe I should explain about my lack of trust, then if you're willing, we can move forward."

"I'm willing to listen." Her face relaxed, the scowl disappeared. The delicate hand he continued to hold flexed and lay limp within his.

"Four years ago, my wife Beth, Marcus's mother, obtained assistance from a lov…friend and left us. She packed her bags while Marcus was at school. No note just left. She was found later in a hotel room, overdosed on alcohol and fentanyl." His stomach muscles tightened. "Someone helped her, a person close to me."

He leaned against the sofa. "It's a relief to tell you. I thought, maybe you'd heard rumors. Some people know all the ugly details. I wanted to make sure you got the truth from me."

"I'm sorry for your loss. I understand. Regardless how much time has passed the betrayal still hurts." She settled against him with their arms touching.

"Veronica and I went to events together because she's so self-centered I never had to worry about trusting or committing to a relationship. But with you, God, with you I'm terrified. Part of me wants to run and part of me wants to let you into my life."

"Oh, Rob." Tears gathered in her eyes.

"What do you say? Do you want to try and make a go of it, to pursue a relationship?"

Chapter 12

On Sunday morning MK rose before dawn. Much to Lee Snyder's dismay newly installed black out blinds blocked him from his needed dose of voyeurism. Dressed in warm gear, she clutched a messenger bag stuffed with papers. Where was she going?

An ugly canine rushed from the house. Lee didn't move, taking slow shallow breaths, he observed her play with the dog. She threw the ball a short distance. The strange beast retrieved the orb and dropped the slimy plastic in front of her. If she hadn't leaned over to wipe some of the excess goo, she may have caught a glimpse of him. With a nimble step, he slipped behind a larger tree. If he showed himself, literally, she'd have him arrested. He assumed the protective order issued was active, and very possibly a new warrant for his arrest entered the system. A misunderstanding, she didn't recognize true love.

Bored with watching the dog fetch, he recalled the glorious spring day he met MK. The day he realized she loved him. He'd delivered a bouquet of flowers. "I love them," she'd said. He knew she really meant she loved him and was embarrassed to say.

One time he had to plow his fist into the new employee's face. Only Lee delivered flowers to her. The kid, Ricky, ended up with a broken arm. Dumb jock. On that very day, he'd paid an exorbitant amount of money to watch her recent release. She'd used him as a model for the hero. Celebrities should be together. Her real-life hero. He puffed out his chest. Her perfume, implanted in his senses, and an urgent desire to touch her shiny blonde hair kept him awake at night.

After release from lockup, he'd stood across the street, from her friend's building, waiting for her to reappear. He'd followed her from the 46th street building and got the opportunity. He grabbed her arm and pulled her into an alley, so people wouldn't stare. A little rough with shoving her against the brick wall, his knife cut, and blood seeped from her throat exciting him. In control, he'd knocked her around, all-the-better for doing so, and if the fag and cop hadn't interrupted, he could have emptied onto her.

Who would have guessed the guy was so strong? If he'd chosen a different alley he could have gotten away. With priors he had to do time. In jail, he'd written several love letters, although he wasn't allowed to post them. He lost his job and didn't miss that, but he did miss her. Soon they'd be forever together.

He took pride in being dedicated to her and patient enough to wait. As expected, the tracker he'd dropped into the fag's luggage led him straight to her house. Incomprehensible, she'd chosen to live in the wilderness of Indiana. He'd take her to the city where they could blend. He finished the cigarette. A God-damn Indian, riding a horse, stopped in front of her backdoor. She ran to him, exhilaration brightening her face. She was happy to see him, a red man. Chief leaned over and kissed her directly on the mouth. What the hell!

Lee started forward, then hesitated. He smashed the cigarette into the ground. Determined to show the whore who was the master, he slunk into the woods.

****

McCartney jerked, stepped away and wiped her mouth. "What a surprise greeting." At the hurt look on his face, she punched his arm. "Great day to ride in a car. Ready?"

Cotton Ball snorted as if he didn't approve of the kiss either. Mac formulated a "Dear John" statement in her head, one that would not hurt Seattle's feelings. The man didn't take rejection well, but before she could speak with elegance and ease, he slid from the horse.

Seattle clasped her arms and drew her into an embrace. "Mac."

Shocked she jumped, bumping hard into Cotton Ball. The equine retreated, and Scat barked in a I'm-hurt-kind-of-way. The man had passion, but she couldn't, wouldn't accept his advances.

"You've a dog." His voice returned to the flat annoyingly precise tone.

Scat sat on her feet. She patted him. His body shook. His rapid heartbeat concerned her. "My friend has a dog, and I've been given the job to raise it, him. His name's Scat."

"He's part wolf?" His voice exploded with anger.

"Yes, and part collie, sheepdog, poodle some kind of mix but certainly fifty percent wolf." She rubbed Scat's ear. "Listen, about the kiss—"

"Where would he get such a dog?"

"Off the internet, but—"

"I'd like to have details. The mixing of a wild creature with a domestic for entertainment must be stopped." Full-blown fury changed Seattle's mild-mannered persona to raging bull.

Crap, the man wouldn't let her finish a sentence. Hands on her hips, she narrowed her eyes. "Okay, not illegal in the city to have this type of dog."

"Maybe not illegal, but unethical." He patted his mount. Cotton Ball wandered to the corral for a bite of late seasonal grass or weeds.

"Ethics didn't play into it. My friend wanted a dog and liked Scat. I'd think you'd be happy he has a home where he's able to be closer to his natural habitat."

His shoulders tightened, and he clamped his jaws. He shifted his narrow-eyed battle glance, making her side-step. "I'll get your email address and have the information sent to you. Are you ready to go?"

She put Scat inside the house. After setting the alarm, she walked to her car. The door was open, and Seattle had strapped into the passenger seat. "Should Cotton Ball roam free?"

"He will stay."

Due to the unexpected lip smack, she must tell Seattle she had started a relationship with Rob; however, his snarl didn't welcome a conversation, business or personal. *Chicken!*

After a quiet extensive drive to the village, she parted ways with Seattle. Not enthusiastic about tutoring, she started the lesson with Caedmon. He wasn't into the session either as he narrowed his slanted dark brown eyes, stood, paced, then returned to the chair.

Three hours had passed, she decided to end the training. "Excellent, Caedmon, you exceeded the free trial exam. I'm confident you'll pass with flying colors. Are you nervous about the performance tests?" He avoided direct eye contact, and his words didn't match his evasiveness.

"I've arranged for you to meet with the director of the testing board on Monday. You'll need to confirm the policies before starting the test. You'll have the next five days to cover any material for the multiple choice on Tuesday. Do you've any questions about the process?"

"No." He hissed and closed his eyelids, but not before she glimpsed his exasperation. He looked at her and bit his lip.

"The next opportunity is in July." Why was he so anxious? "Have you flown in an airplane before?"

"Yes. I've been reading about air flight and velocity. I'm excited to apply the knowledge." His eyes glittered.

"Terrific, you'll fly home Tuesday night, and I'll stay another day to spend time with my daughter. Do you think you'll have any trouble traveling by yourself?" Mac walked toward the door, wanting to leave and finish a chapter before bed.

"He won't, because I'm going with you." Seattle's monotone growl came from behind her.

She pivoted and gave him a wide-eyed stare. "Are you going to go throughout the city and find mutant wolves to release back into the wild?"

"No, I simply wanted to visit New York and," he pulled her outside, "spend time alone with you."

She disengaged. "I need to tell you that I'm involved with—"

"Seattle, I need to talk to you right now." A woman, she'd seen him with before, demanded. Her long brown hair, twisted into an attractive messy knot, bounced as she talked. The pink knit top beneath a lightweight fall jacket showed an inch or more of her skin before the low-hip-riding jeans melded to her long legs.

"Jennifer, can it wait? I'm getting ready to take Mac

home."

Her head lowered, and she nodded. "I'll come to your house, later."

John Blackhawk rushed into the group, barely stopping before crashing into Seattle. "Need you." He leaned over and placed his hands on top of his knees and tried to catch his breath. "Problem with mine, come quickly, need help."

A dusting of soot covered his face. The smell of pencil lead surrounded him, leading her to assume he'd been in the mine.

Caedmon ran from the community building. "What's going on?"

"I'm not sure. John, has anyone been injured?"

"Cave in. Hear voices. Hurry, limited time."

Chapter 13

Mac paced in front of Gate Seven and tightened her grip on her cellphone. They were to board the plane in two minutes and there wasn't a sign of Seattle or Caedmon. She cursed all men. They complain about women being late. Maybe they had trouble getting through security?

"Mac!"

Caedmon and Seattle jogged to the waiting line. She sensed the stress that surrounded them. "Our row will be called in a moment. Is everything okay at the village?"

Seattle nodded. "Yes, the miners were extracted. A few breaks, minor bruises and cuts. Engineering's involved and will review the cave-in. I want to thank you for your help." Travelers surrounded them. "It looks like we need to move."

Caedmon and Mac were seated side-by-side with Seattle taking the window seat. Despite the turbulence, she concentrated on the project. After she extracted as much information as possible about the cave-in, they reviewed strategies for the test.

"Caedmon, I talked to the test coordinator and found out about the Pro Bono Scholar. Will you be able to stay in New York and contribute your last semester providing free legal services?"

"Yes, Mac, I've done everything possible to make it work, and I've friends in New York who I can stay with."

Seattle appeared to be in a deep sleep.

"Why haven't you mentioned this before? Does the council know you won't be there for three or so months?"

"No. You cannot tell them. I'll provide service for my tribe. The patent can be registered in New York as well as Indiana. I need to use the restroom." He sprinted the length of the aisle.

The confession made her uneasy. She didn't trust Caedmon. He lied to his family, community, and he unceasingly lied to her by holding onto the skeleton in the closet. She touched Seattle's forearm, resisting the urge to tell him everything. She needed more evidence. "We're landing in New York. You've been asleep since take off, are you okay?"

He yawned and straightened. "Yes, I'm fine." He pierced her with a stare. "I don't need to remind you to keep the alternative fuel source confidential."

Aha. I'd guessed correctly. "No. Not that I'm aware of the complexity of the formula but I know of its value to the world and your people, I'll protect the intelligence."

As expected, Seattle grinned.

Caedmon returned to his seat. The wheels hit pavement, and a short time later Mac waited while passengers rushed to obtain their carry-ons and deboard. After gathering their bags, she led them through the crowded airport. "My friend said he'd meet us at the pick-up zone." Hopefully, Xavier would be on time to collect them. They walked outside into the sun.

"Xavier!" She waved at him. He stood by the door of a sleek black limo. She dropped her bag, hugged and kissed him. It felt like years, instead of weeks, since she'd seen him.

Xavier's gargantuan smile stayed in place as he lifted her bag.

"Please meet my friends, Dr. Seattle Coyote and Caedmon Star."

"Xavier Montague, at your service." He motioned for the driver to load their bags.

Caedmon smiled. "It's nice to meet you, Mr. Montague, I've heard a lot about you. Thank you for arranging transportation."

Seattle nodded. "Nice to meet you."

Bags loaded; they climbed into the car.

"Seattle, Mac didn't tell me why you were visiting the city, especially during the off season. On vacation?"

"Right, I'm on vacation." Seattle settled against the leather seat.

"You're a doctor of what?" Xavier asked.

"Ph.D. in chemistry, biochemistry. Do you know much about biochemistry?" Seattle's arrogant intonation raised her suspicious fears. She should've expected the topic to arise, just not this early.

"Can't say that I do." Xavier glanced at her.

"Mr. Montague, I understand you purchased a pet which is half wolf. I'd like to have the information about the people you obtained him from."

Mac swallowed hard and murmured, "Seattle, stop."

"What's wrong with having a wolf as a pet? Scat was content to be in the city, but he's happier at Mac's country house." Xavier's back stiffened. "BTW, who's watching him?"

"You don't know what is wrong with taking a natural predator whose soul existence was to maintain the balance of nature and make it into a pet? Force it to conform to your rules and standards, to fight against its very instinct?" Seattle glared at him.

"Seattle." She tapped Xavier's arm. "Boy next door. You'll probably have to buy a few new sneakers."

"Where's the guy guarding you? Roberto or something?"

"What—"

"Misspoke." Xavier cleared his throat. "The doctor's right. At the time I purchased him, I was thinking of myself and not of Scat's internal instincts. I guess that is why I rushed to bring him to your house. I knew he would be happier in or closer to nature." He nodded. "It was wrong of me to buy a wolf, even part-wolf and try to make it conform to my lifestyle. I'll be more than happy to share the seller's information. Also, other websites I viewed, before I purchased him."

Seattle nodded. "Thank you, Mr. Montague."

"Absolutely." Xavier removed his arm from around her. "Mac, do you have pages for me?"

"Yes." She dug into her carryon and removed a thick packet. "Are you and Noah still dating?"

He took the envelope. "He's coming to visit next weekend and later for an extended visit. You'll help me narrow a list of activities?"

"Sure, when we meet with Cassie for lunch."

Xavier glanced at his watch. "Great! Here we are. I'm going to toss you out of the car, because I'm late for an appointment." He squished his face in a comical sympathy expression. "Have a nice visit, Caedmon and Seattle. I'll send all the information about Scat's lineage in an email to Mac, and she'll forward. Ta Ta."

Mac waved. "I've arranged for connecting rooms. We've approximately thirty minutes before Caedmon is to meet with Smith, the director."

They unpacked and caught a cab with seconds to spare. "We're going to the café next door and wait for you. Good luck." Mac smiled.

Caedmon nodded and walked into the building.

Seattle played with his spoon, flipping it over. He'd been quiet for the past twenty minutes as they sipped coffee and ate flaky croissants. Mac pressed his spoon to the table. "Okay, tell me what's bothering you."

"You still don't remember meeting me?

"It's very clear in my mind, a couple of months ago you woke me from a sound sleep, and we had a rocky start." She crossed her arms.

He shook his head. "Two years ago, Dog's house."

She closed her eyes, trying to recapture images of people she'd met during that time. "I'm sorry, I don't recall." She blinked. *Oh no, the repairman.*

He scowled. "Yes, I can tell you do remember."

"Typically, I'm a friendly person. Unfortunately, on that day I'd been given negative reviews for Surviving Queens, and I learned I had a violent fan following me. To be honest, you didn't put in any effort at being nice."

"You soaked me with the kitchen sprayer."

"You came from under the sink and gawked at me."

"I thought you were pretty, that first impression didn't last long."

"You accused me of using Forest Dog to get confidential information."

"You were."

"Why didn't you mention this during the dozens of times we rode to the village?"

"I'm so pumped. Mr. Smith gave me some great pointers about the test tomorrow. Come on, let's go. I want to start reviewing right now." Caedmon stood beside their table. He pushed his eyeglasses higher on his nose and flipped through a booklet.

"Sure, I'm dedicated to helping you and your people." Mac jumped from her chair, grabbed her purse and rushed toward the door.

"Caedmon, it's nearly one in the morning. It's normal for you to be nervous, however, you need to get some rest, or you'll be sluggish." Exhausted from travel and the odd comment Xavier made about Rob she couldn't wait to take a shower and rest. First, she had to get these two out of her room. Caedmon paced. Seattle, in the adjoining room with the connecting door wide open, had the television on full volume.

Caedmon paused in his pivot and frowned. "Do you hear someone knocking, or am I losing it?"

"I didn't hear anything, but I'll check." She uncrossed her legs; pins and needles jettisoned her gait. Bent, she made her way to the door. "Who is it?"

"It's Rob."

She threw the safety latch; spring loaded it banged the door. "Hi, what a surprise."

"What's wrong with you?" He entered and scanned the room.

She viewed the tableau from his sightline. A young man with jogging pants and a t-shirt was sprawled across her bed. Boxes of Chinese carry-out, reeking of tangy sweet scents, were scattered about the tabletops. A partially dressed brooding Seattle Coyote leaned against the door frame. A country music song, about a scorned lover, played in the background. Yes, the scene looked scandalous, but her priority was to get an explanation about the probable guarding of her.

Rob pressed his back to the closed door. "What's going on?"

"Pins and needles in lower legs, because I sat in one position for so long. Rob Barringer, I'd like you to meet Caedmon Star, a young man I've been tutoring, and Seattle Coyote a squirely guardian of the mentee. Guys, Rob Barringer." She forced her legs to remain straight.

"Seattle, how are you? Caedmon nice to meet you. Doesn't explain what's going on in here?" He dropped his duffle bag on the floor.

Mac glanced at Seattle and then Rob.

"Caedmon, we're finished for the night."

As Caedmon gathered his notes, Seattle faced Rob. "For the past several weeks, Mac has been preparing Caedmon to pass a bar exam. A rush because we can't wait later than February. He'll become an attorney and help us with legal processes. Early tomorrow he'll begin the NY bar exam, then he'll take the Indiana Bar Exam. I'm sure he'll be successful. Now, it's late. Mac, we'll see you early in the morning."

"Yes, sleep well." Mac shuffled to the connecting door.

Caedmon said, "Akitês."

"Don't be sorry. Akya'tatho', wi'yu', tetwatahnuóhkwa'." Seattle paused. "Fate has intervened."

"Yes. Love is meant to be shared. Destiny will take its course," Caedmon replied.

What did he mean? Mac considered asking, instead slowly shut the door and the lock clicked. She collected notes strewn across the bed and smoothed out the covers. Assumptions are horrible, but a fact of life. In the future, she needed to engage and be more direct.

"You're so unpredictable. Why didn't you tell me about Caedmon?" Arms crossed, legs braced, he hadn't moved away from the door. His low, controlled, voice tone didn't give leave to his temperament.

"The Indian council expected the mentoring to be classified. Each Sunday morning, Seattle escorts me to the village. I'd strategize and develop lesson plans for Caedmon, who's extremely bright, a genius. I understood their conditions, honored their wishes and signed a non-disclosure agreement." She gathered the various food containers and dumped them into the trashcan. "As I would honor yours if you had a secret. Maybe one that involved me."

His silence made her turn and look. Would their fragile beginning already be fraught with mistrust? He didn't say why his wife left him. Why did Xavier say Robert was protecting her?

The television, in the adjoining room, turned off, creating an uncomfortable silence.

"I was hoping for a 'I'm glad to see you. It'll be great to spend a couple of days together.' " Displeasure infiltrated his blue eyes. She smiled. If he was angry, it meant that he cared.

"Of course, I'm glad to see you." She sashayed toward him, tugged him toward the tiny sofa. "I'm just surprised to see you, in my New York hotel room, at one in the morning." She frowned. "How did you get the room number?"

"My son, who is taking care of your beast." He removed his hat and threw it onto the tabletop. "I've a meeting with the New York Mounted Police Department. They're adding a hundred equine police to their force. My horses are the best for police training, you know, for crowd control and criminal pursuit. I meet with them tomorrow."

Rob clasped her hand, caressed her palm with his thumb. "Why New York? Shouldn't he have taken the exam in Indiana?"

"He wanted to pass the NY Bar, a goal. He thought it was a more difficult exam. He said that if he passed it, the Indiana would be a cake walk." She released her hand and caught his glance. "I'm happy for you, about the horse patrol deal. That's wonderful, Rob. Why didn't you tell me?"

"Tell you what?"

"Xavier told me you are protecting me." She swallowed. "I thought what we had was real."

He sighed and sat on the sofa. "Please sit beside me, and I'll explain."

She sat in the corner and crossed her legs. He inched toward her and pried her hand from its tight grip on her trousers. "What I feel for you is real and unexpected. I haven't been close to a woman in a decade."

She uncrossed her legs. "Why did Xavier say you're guarding me?"

He entwined his fingers with hers. "Because in addition to managing a ranch, I work for Bolton's Valor Security and Investigations. One of the owners is Vince Samuels."

"Xavier's cousin." She didn't dare glance into his dreamy eyes and possibly see pity.

"Yes. Your dear friend hired the company, me, to provide protection for you. At first, I didn't think you needed anyone as you're a strong intelligent female who can hold her own, then I found cigarette butts outside your house."

Anxiety took root in the pit of her stomach. The Chinese food churned, threatening to return. *He's found me.*

"You need to cover your bathroom window."

"I know, already did it."

"Matt called and said he was to meet you and evaluate your barn. We went inside and discovered someone's camping out." The concerned look in his eyes directly contrasted with his calm voice tone.

She leaned forward and grasped for breath. "This can't be happening again. I've made a mistake and let my guard down."

Rob tugged her close and pressed her head onto his chest. "Sometimes it helps to get a grip by talking through the problem."

"Two years ago, a crazy fan attacked me. He never knew my real name, but always called me by my pen name, MK. Why isn't he in jail?"

"His name is?"

"Lee Snyder. He sent letters, e-mails and then baskets." She coughed, trying to open her throat. "He made references to what I was wearing, the smell of my perfume, and my location. Xavier took me to the police station; I filed for a protection order. A strange man with a simple name who thinks he knows everything and wants to be somebody special. He delivered flowers, which is how he got closer to me. Xavier and I submitted papers and notes in addition to any baskets as evidence. The detective told me if I ignored Snyder, he'd find someone else to bother. He didn't."

She pushed a bit of hair behind her ear. "He made threats and demanded to be seen together in public. I didn't know this person. At the peak of my career, I received a lot of flowers. I couldn't describe the delivery guy to the police." She took a deep breath.

"In his mind, he believed I accepted his advances. I notified the police of the threats. Snyder sent a note stating he'd kill me or Cassie if I didn't revoke the order and publicly acknowledge him. A copy of a photo from a magazine spread was delivered, and a circle had been drawn around a face in the background. Snyder was a couple of feet away. Finally, I had a face to go with the name. Xavier and I went back to the detective and demanded I have police protection."

Rob kissed her creased brow. "What did they do?"

"The protective order was extended; however, until an act of violence has been committed, it's difficult to get an arrest. I was to keep my eyes open, and if I spotted him within fifty feet of me, I could call them. I attended talent events with bodyguards. I became a recluse and imposed restrictions on my daughter. The new time constraints imposed on her made her angry. I wanted, needed, her to be aware and to be safe. A documentary idea, based on Forest Dog, was given to me. I thought it would be a great way to escape the city and for the next six months I researched and wrote. Cassie enjoyed the time away from New York, but this is her home. She missed her friends and wanted to be in a school setting again."

She snuggled against his shoulder. "I didn't hear anything else from Snyder until spring two years ago. One day, Xavier and I left his apartment, and he stopped next door to get a coffee. Lee Snyder attacked me using a knife. He dragged me into an alcove and pricked my neck. Blood trickled along my throat and chest when Xavier arrived with a policeman in tow."

"What happened to Snyder?" He rubbed the top of her hand, soothing circles much like when he calmed the horse in the stall the first day they met.

"He'd previously attacked another woman, a porn star, which should not have influenced her case. However, Snyder got probation and later the criminal act was expunged. With my case, the district attorney was vying for a better position and wanted aggressive action taken against crime. Snyder's a sociopath. This time he couldn't convince the jury of his innocence. With a prior arrest and his attack on me, he went to prison. He must be out. I need to call Cassie."

"Where is she?"

"Here, in a boarding facility. She's safe and sound in New York City." Her voice wobbled. "Please be safe."

"It's almost two, put your fear to rest and send her a text. Tomorrow we'll go to her dorm and to the police station. In the meantime, you should rest."

She must look as exhausted as she felt. After sending a text, she could not let go of the device. "Yes, thank you."

Rob stood. "I want a relationship built on trust and communication. Without trust we've lust and little else. Not that I'm complaining about lust by any means."

"Ditto. You could have told me about your job." Self-conscious, she admitted most of her life had been exposed. Did he regret their relationship? "My promise was to protect the Native Americans." She lifted her feet, the slippers dropped off, and she lay on the bed. "In the future I'll share all intel with you, if you share with me. Deal?"

"Deal." He laid beside her, took her hand into his. "Do you want me to stay here tonight?"

"Yes," she whispered as if voicing her pleasure would curse her future.

"She's safe, Mac."

Chapter 14

Unwashed bodies, reeking of sweat, liquor and vomit engulfed the police station entrance. Two lucky detainees were chained to chairs, three females hovered against the walls. Seattle coughed and held his hand over his nose and mouth. She blew out a breath, while ignoring Rob who insisted she tell Seattle about Snyder.

"May I help you?" Dressed in blue, Sue was written across the name badge. No doubt they resembled an odd group: one striking Native American with sharp cheekbones and coal black eyes, one gorgeous rancher from hat to authentically well-worn boots, and her–a pale shaking woman wearing a cream tinted designer pant suit and matching overcoat.

She wanted to make a statement. Experience had provided a foundation, the best way to get attention was to act with authority and dress the part. "We need to see Detective Rider, please."

"Who should I say wants to see him?" As if specimens under a microscope, Sue ran her gage along each of them.

Mac lifted her chin a notch. "McCartney James, I'm also known as MK."

"Regarding?" Sharp and short. Sue wasn't a lily, rather a coneflower strong and able to withstand the elements.

"Protective Order 43C03-1812-PO-005361." A

long number and one she'd never forget. She brought the Protective Order case number notification on her cellphone and turned the screen toward Officer Congeniality.

Sue typed, a few seconds later they were shown to a conference room. Shortly thereafter a stout silver-haired man with a beak nose, small mouth, a shiny badge clipped to his belt and a pistol lodged in a holster strapped across his shoulder sauntered into the room.

"Mac, it's nice to see you." His voice was laced with exhaustion. Lines creased the outside of his eyes and dark shadows indicated he unrelentingly dedicated most of his time helping and protecting people.

"As with you, Blake. I don't want to waste your time, so I'll be direct. Has Lee Snyder been released from prison?" She couldn't sit in a chair, instead paced.

"Yes, due to overcrowding and good behavior he's been given early release." He glanced at his notebook. "Three weeks ago."

"Is he in New York?" Rob inquired. "Why wasn't she notified?"

"And you are?"

"I'm Rob Barringer, a friend and neighbor of Ms. James. And this is Seattle Coyote, another friend."

"A few days ago, he failed to report to his parole officer. There's a warrant issued."

"Why wasn't I notified?" She forced her legs to stop moving.

Rob took her hand and entwined their fingers. "It's possible, probable, Lee Snyder has been staying in Mac's barn in Lantern, Indiana. The local police are currently searching the area. Does he go by an alias?"

Blake shook his head. "Generally, fanatics like this

want the attention and use their name, desiring the association with the victim. I'll contact the police force in Indiana and give them details. Thank you for alerting us. If you don't have any more questions, I've appointments."

"I gave them a cigarette butt for DNA, but it'll take weeks to process."

"Good, that'll help in court." The detective bustled from the room.

"That's it? I'll give them details." Seattle swore in his native tongue. She caught bastard, but the rest was lost in translation.

Mac sighed. "I know it's frustrating. There's nothing we can we do from this standpoint."

"You seem to be calmer," Rob said. "I'm surprised about how well you're handling the situation."

"I'm protected, because I'm with you." She glanced at them. "Both of you. If Cassandra's at school and out of harm's way, my worry is less."

"Let's get out of here. Have you heard from her?" Rob held open the door.

"No, she hasn't replied to my text. She was going out with a friend and planned a late night. Now, she's in class for the day. I'll give her a call." She removed her cellphone from the carryall and followed the guys from the building.

"Voicemail and answering machine, I left a message at her dorm room and on her phone."

"What now?" Seattle scoured the streets.

"Rob's been to New York before, but this is your first visit. If you wanted to see one sight, what would it be?"

"Pizza Pi or Skywalk Diner in New Jersey." He

blurted, keenly interested in his boots or the checkered floor.

Mac didn't understand. They could eat at any of the wonderful and famous New York restaurants. "This is significant to you?"

"I'm a fan of a crime show. We need to eat lunch somewhere. It'd be nice to see the locations which were often seen on the series if they're still around. Maybe stop by J's Bake Shop where Kris shot the guy in the foot. Get cannoli." Seattle winked. "Of course, I'd rather go to Big Bing, a dance club where the wise guys used to hang out. It's really called the Smooth Dolls, and it's also located in Jersey."

Mac smiled, sidled beside him and nudged. He double stepped. "Coyote your prismatic-constantly-evolving-self never ceases to amaze me. What time's your appointment with the horse patrol guy, Rob?"

"In ten minutes, it'll take about an hour. You two go ahead, and I'll catch up." Rob pulled her close. "It'll be all right. I'll call you for a location after I'm finished."

"We'll go to Skywalk Diner, and then J's Bake Shop." Seattle's happy expression resembled a kid who'd received a special gift. He hailed a cab. "I'll take care of her, Rob."

"Ok, I'll call." Rob kissed her, then climbed into the town car pulling close to the curb.

One hour and thirty minutes later Mac tried to call Cassie again. No answer. She could be anywhere, in class or a store. The table at J's Bake Shop was covered by a red and white vinyl cloth with beige salt and pepper shakers as center pieces. When her cellphone rang, she jumped, hitting Seattle's plate as she dived into her bag. His half-eaten cannoli went flying to the edge of the table. He caught the treat before it landed on the floor.

"Okay, we'll see you at the hotel." She disconnected and glanced at Seattle. "Caedmon's finished for the day. He's on his way to the hotel." Her stomach knotted. When would Cassie call? A horrible premonition kept racing through her thoughts.

Rob exited a black car as they were leaving J's. "We need to return to the hotel," she said.

He tapped the side of the car. "We need to go to the city, downtown."

They arrived at the hotel and met Caedmon in the lobby.

"It went well?" Seattle asked.

"Yes. I'm sure I passed the exams today. I need to get through Tuesday, and I'll be home free. Could we get something to eat?" Caedmon's thin body wavered as he stepped forward.

"Sure, you guys go ahead." She glanced at Rob. "I'm going to Cassie's dorm room, maybe she's on a lunch break."

"I'm going with Mac," Rob said.

Her mobile rang as they exited the hotel lobby. Excitement rose in her chest when the cell ID indicated Cassie's dorm room landline.

"Hi, Mrs. James, this is Katlin, Cassie's roommate."

"Yes, I remember, Katlin, how are you? Just a second, I can't hear over the street noise. I'm going into the lobby. I've tried to reach Cassie. Do you know where she is?"

"Yes, at your house. She had a fight with her boyfriend and decided to travel to Indiana early for the holidays. I guess she forgot you were coming to New York."

"Thanks, Katlin, I appreciate your call." Mac plopped onto a high-back chair. Her purse fell with a clunk to the floor. She rocked, gripping her churning belly.

"What is it? What's wrong?" Rob asked. She rubbed her stomach. "Talk to me." He placed his hand on her back and rubbed smooth circular patterns.

"Cassie's at my house. The attacker has been or is at my house. My God, she's alone and doesn't know anyone. What will I do?" She starred at the cellphone, tightly gripped in her hand. Her thoughts jumbled. A sharp shooting pain rumbled around, piercing her chest. "She isn't answering."

Rob touched her shoulder. "I've got people who will help."

"Good, will you please call them? Her phone might not be working." She pressed the security app. "My security system if offline."

"I'll call the Sheriff and Luke. He can be there in five minutes tops. Pack and we'll leave as soon as possible." Rob drew her out of the chair, and they went to her hotel room.

"Luke's not answering." Rob dialed his house number. "Marcus, is your grandfather there?"

"He went on a date with the widow." Rob turned away, and his voice lowered. "I understand it blows. You're not going out late at night while I'm in New York and there's a snowstorm predicted. Your friends can wait."

Mac shoved clothes into her weekend bag, while focusing on his conversation.

"Listen carefully, Marcus, Mac has a dangerous man following her, and he might be at her place. Her daughter, Cassandra, is there. Did Luke leave you the widow's number? It's imperative for him to get the girl and take her to our house. I wish your grandfather would move into the twenty-first century and get a cellphone."

"We'll leave a message for her that Luke will pick her up. Have him call when she's safe, okay son?" He paused. "The attacker might be there. Yes, I know I can trust you to take care of it. I know you're an adult. Bye Marcus, I'll see you in a few hours." Rob pressed the face of his cellphone, swiping left.

"I've changed into my travel clothes, so I'm ready. Were you able to reach the police?" Without waiting for an answer, she ran to the hotel phone and dialed the concierge. "What's the telephone number for Midwest Airlines?" She wrote down the ten digits, then turned toward Rob.

"Marcus will call Luke. I'll try them again; it rang to the number wheel." He held her close. "She'll be okay, Mac. He wants you, so he won't harm her. They can be there in minutes. It'll all work out. Call her cellphone again, leave a message that my father will get her and take her to my house."

****

MK's daughter shunned caution. An unlocked door became a direct invitation to enter the house. Lee left the door ajar and listened to the ear shattering music. His father always told him when the ear bursting music would get them evicted, followed by a smack to the head. The bruise usually lasted three days, unlike the other beatings inflicted by the madman. His mother, a disciple of God, tried to protect him. MK reminded him of his mama, another reason for them to be together. Forever. In life or death.

The girl unpacked her luggage, swaying to a popular contemporary tune, wiping out any negative energy occupying the space. "Young, beautiful, and free, that's what I am," she sang.

The lights flashed off. She stopped singing as the song ended. Accustomed to traffic, people noise, and bright lights twenty-four seven she should be afraid. She rubbed her arms. A quick shift into the bathroom, he remained hidden keeping a visual of her through the crack of the door.

Three candles and a box of matches thumped against the tabletop in the bedroom. She lightly stepped over to the bed and rummaged through a backpack. A mobile phone lit the space. "Two bars and ten voicemails. Hum, voicemails or mother."

Lee slipped into the hallway and braced his back against the wall.

"Your mailbox is full." The robotic voice announced. The girl rummaged in her bag. "Arggh, where's the charger?"

The deafening quiet prevented him from moving from the hallway. Suddenly tree branches beat against the window and the blasted wind brought down a torrent of hail.

The strike of a match candles brightened the room, and the scent of sulfur infiltrated his nostrils. Lee removed a cigarette from his jacket pocket and placed the stick in his mouth. He sucked in the satisfying tobacco aroma, then stuffed the unlit cig into his pocket. After he secured the little missy, he'd light the smoke.

She pirouetted to the other side of the room, humming a ballad, and placed an antique comb and brush set on top of the dresser. The floors creaked as he shifted.

She stopped singing and pivoted, facing the door. He stiffened.

A moment later she performed the battement tendu, with one leg stretched out and slid the other foot along the floor until the foot was fully articulated toes pointed. He could not move, instead remained standing near the door, watching her graceful quick little jumps until she bumped into a dresser.

"Ouch." She peered into the mirror. Fear of the unknown, he knew it well, had paralyzed her.

The guy was medium to tall build, broad shoulders like one would imagine a woodsman looked like, blond hair and clear blue eyes. His smile made deep dimples appear on each side of his mouth. A pretty boy grin reached his eyes, which pissed Lee off. The impromptu dance show was only for him, not some randy teen. Lee rounded the corner, out of sight, although within hearing. A hallway mirror gave him a perfect view of the two.

The guy uncrossed his arms and pushed away from the door frame. "Hello, Cassie, I'm Marcus Barringer, a friend and neighbor of your mother."

"How? How did you get in?"

"The door was unlocked." He narrowed his eyes. "And open."

Emotions crossed her face as if she tried to remember. "No, little MK, you left the door unlocked and didn't reset the alarm."

Barringer shook his head. "Didn't she call and tell you my grandfather would be coming to get you?"

"My phone's dead and no electricity, so no recharge. Where's your grandfather?" Mini-MK was smart enough to glance out the window.

The boy stared in Lee's direction. He took a step

farther into the shadows, entered his love's bedroom and watched the teens through the sliver of space between the door and frame. MK's floral perfume and clean fresh linen, coconut shampoo and citrus scented potpourri surrounded him, distracted him. He'd broken into her New York apartment and the familiar scents, unique to her, became orgasmic. He'd stolen one of her scarves and occasionally tied the silk around his neck. Damn the police who came and took all his tokens.

"I came instead. We should go. When we get into the truck you can recharge your cell or use mine and call your mother."

She didn't move.

"We need to go, now."

He looked innocent enough. Yet, why would MK send a young man to get her precious? Lee smiled. MK knew he'd found her hidey-hole.

"Ok." She pretended to throw items into a backpack, grabbed pepper spray and the keys for the car rental. She slid the spray into her hand and twisted the container.

Snyder silently laughed.

Chapter 15

"What's the delay?" Mac paced in front of the large windows, overlooking the tarmac. The flood of canceled flight announcements interrupted his response.

"Come and sit, you'll use all your energy on steps." Rob tapped the empty seat beside him. "Your friend was confident she could get us on a flight. We'll be home in less than two hours after takeoff."

Cold fear coursed in her veins. Horrible violent scenarios looped through her head. She sat on the hard seat and rested her head on his shoulder, comforted by being able to lean on someone. Why couldn't she turn off the negative thoughts?

Rob chuckled. "Moxie Maggie is an interesting woman, assertive yet classy creates a unique person."

"You sound like a professional, zeroing in on a person's character." She laughed.

Tell her you know every little detail about her! If she finds out, she'll hate you. Tell her about your past and dad. But it's more than that…

"But, yes, she's one of a kind. I first came to the city fresh out of college, and she interviewed me for a job at a law firm as a para legal. She plainly told me I was as green as the grass growing in Central Park. She took a chance by offering a low paying position to read and edit. I'd graduated with an English degree and hoped to pursue a career in the legal world. Research's my

144

interest. A few weeks pregnant with Cassie, two previous opportunities failed because I told the truth. Maggie didn't care. She's an inspiration, a mentor and confidant."

"Cassie's father didn't help with her care?"

"Cassie's father, Kurt Miller, and I didn't marry. We were on our way to St. Patrick's Church, to see Father John for pre-marital counseling when a semi-trailer truck hit the drivers' side of our car. Kurt was instantly killed. I didn't have a seatbelt on as I'd turned to grab a stack of thank you notes in the backseat. They were unique, and I couldn't wait to show him. My foot opened the door when the collision occurred, and I flew. I was released from the hospital with a broken arm, several stitches and a baby in my belly. I thanked God, as Kurt will always be a part of my memories. The vicious looking scar near my right shoulder is a constant reminder about how uncertain and valuable life is." She paused and glanced into his face. "You've never mentioned the scar, why?"

He rubbed the marred shoulder. "I never considered it an issue. I was more aware of you as a beautiful sensitive person. At the dance you made it appear as if you were an unwed mother."

"I am. Not that I'm condoning pre-marital sex, but we were going to be married in two days. Cassie had surrogate fathers in Xavier and my father, when he was alive." Her voice softened. "Maggie is her Godmother and teaches her about life from her own," she chuckled, "perspective."

"You're very proud of her."

"She's brilliant. It's interesting how personalities are molded because of genes and environment. At times I'll see be a bit of Cassie's father in her, especially when she becomes stubborn, not just in looks or mannerisms, but in the way she evaluates and navigates a situation. She may decide to approach the predicament or project with caution or jump. At other times I see shades of Xavier and Maggie. Maggie took Cassie to her first ballet. From the moment the dancers came onto the stage, she was hooked."

"She's studying ballet at the fine arts college?"

"Yes. It's her first year. I can't wait to see her. It was easy to get together when I lived in the city, but now there's a distance. Must be empty nest syndrome." She tilted her head, listening. "They're calling us to the gate."

****

"You'll see her soon," Rob said, reassuring her.

The azure skies had intermittent white fog shrouded clouds. Turbulence caused the small commuter plane to wobble as it severed a cloud mass. Mac reached for a paper sack, hoping the turmoil roiling within her stomach would settle.

Cassie is safe with Luke.

"The seatbelt light's on, we're close to the airport. Do you need anything, before we close in on the runway?" Rob steadfastly remained a solemn support.

"No, thank you. Sorry for being quiet, I can't get out of my head."

He wrapped his arm across her shoulders. "I wish I could say something else to comfort you."

"Do you think Luke found Cassie?"

"I'm sure he did. We'll make contact the minute we hit the ground. Flooding has elevated from probable to a hundred percent. Your car's at the airport, right?"

"Yes." She peered out the window. Rain and hail slushed from the wings during the decent. The wheels connected with the tarmac, making the plane's sides rattle.

"If we don't make phone contact," he paused, "don't frown at me, the phones might be out of order due to the weather conditions. I'll follow you to your place, then we'll go to mine. If she's not there, she'll be at Luke's."

"Why do you call him Luke?" She reluctantly turned away from the window and calculated the time to get to her house.

"Because he was responsible for the death of my wife," he bluntly replied.

Talk about dropping a bomb. He was serious. Mac ran her fingers lightly over his creased brow and along the side of his face. "What?"

"We've enough on our plate right now, we'll talk later." The harshness of his voice and his tightly corded muscles didn't make her retreat. Underneath the coldness, was a pain, an ache, created from the loss of his wife and father.

"When you're ready, I'll listen."

They attempted to call again. None of them were answering. She watched the clock tick away as they waited to deboard. As with most Midwest storms, driving became treacherous and flooded roads made the trip time consuming. The town of Lantern's security lights beamed, creating an eerie atmosphere and adding to her worries.

Her all-wheel drive vehicle helped her to maneuver through the dime-sized hail and furiously blowing winds. The car lost traction and skidded toward an embankment before she righted the vehicle. Behind her, Rob inched forward, controlling his truck.

The automatic backup generator Matt had installed

worked. Cassie's bedroom light became a symbol of hope. She slammed on the brake. The car slid sideways, she braced for the impact knowing she'd hit the hitching post or end up in the hot springs. A connection with the rail threw her forward into the steering wheel. Her knee rammed into the door. She unfastened the seatbelt, unlatched the door and promptly fell onto the ground.

"Are you hurt?" Rob shouted over the wind as he picked her up.

"Fine." She bit out.

"What the hell. Did you realize the rate of speed you were going as you came around the corner?" The winds continuously blew bitter pieces of ice. Their outpour of emotions, her fear and his anger, hung in the frigid air.

She attempted to shrug off his hands. "Let me go. My daughter."

Simultaneously, they turned and raced toward the house. Rob stopped abruptly and blocked the door. "Let me go in first. I'm sure Luke was able to get her. I just don't want…"

He was right. That's what she told herself the few seconds she stood at the doorway, leaning against the wall to relieve the pain on her knee. She had to know and rushed into the great room. A message loomed large on the wall. Red liquid dripped, pooling on the desk. She wrapped her arms across her waist. She darted into Cassie's room. Papers were strewn throughout, but no sign of her daughter.

"I thought I told you to wait."

She jumped. "I couldn't. She's not here."

"No, I'm sure Luke got to her."

The primary bedroom reeked of perfume and cigarette smoke. Lamps had been overturned and artwork destroyed. A photo had been removed from the frame and torn into particles. She picked up a small portion of the glossy bit. Her and Kurt's wedding announcement. The last image of them as a couple. An ache squeezed her heart. She sat on the quilted comforter, an heirloom passed down from her grandmother. The blanket had been sliced into several pieces and the cotton batting exposed. Some of her clothes had been removed from the closet, cut and distributed around the room. Her limited lingerie had been ripped and littered the floor like confetti. He would not destroy her life. The anger, slow to build, escalated quickly superseding the fear.

"Did you see the message on the wall in the living room? What does it mean?"

"It's a quote from a movie, let's talk about it later. I need to find Cassie," she insisted.

"You must leave everything as it is. The police will take photographs."

"Why aren't the police here? You talked to them over two hours ago; shouldn't they have been here by now?" She swiped at the tears hovering on her cheeks.

"Come on." He took her arm in his and led her from the house. Walking past Cassie's rental car, Rob extracted his cellphone from his jacket pocket and pressed the face. "This is Rob Barringer calling from McCartney James's house. A crime. Yes." A moment passed. "Yes. Thank you."

"You're mine. He'll never leave me alone. His pride has been damaged, and he'll jerk me around until he's gets what he wants. Death?" She stepped on the running board of the truck, then lowered her foot back to the ground and ran to the barn. Rob called her name.

Unheeded, she grasped the metal "I" shaped handle, braced her booted feet in the slush and pulled.

Rob placed his hand on top of hers. "Let me help you."

Together they tugged and opened the door. Limited light filtered through the gap. A slim petite body hung, by a rope, in the middle of the barn.

"Oh my God, not my baby." Mac repeated the mantra as she ran forward.

"Wait!" he shouted. "This could be a trap, center a body in the open, then capture or kill you."

She stopped. He clasped her arm, tugged her backward and whispered, "Let's take our time."

"Okay."

He surveyed the area, released her and together they approached the body, swinging as the wind circulated. Like a rag doll Mac dropped to the straw covered floor in front of the small feet of the plastic figure. She violently sobbed into her hands.

Long blonde hair spun, covering the mannequin's face. Another message. She removed a tissue from her overcoat pocket, wiped her eyes, and blew her nose.

He rubbed her back. "It's not real. He's a twisted fella who hung a look-a-like doll from the rafters."

She stopped thinking and barely breathing rushed to his truck.

****

Rob sat on the driver's seat. A quick connection, he explained the destruction of the house and the body double in the barn to the dispatcher. It only took a few minutes to get to his house. She ran from room to room on the lower level. Rob searched the upper levels.

They met in the foyer. "No one. You?"

"No," she said. "What now?"

"We'll go to Luke's house." Rob held her hand as they hurried along the snow shoveled sidewalk. Five minutes later they arrived at a federal style house.

"Marcus! Luke!" Rob didn't take off his boots at the door.

"We're in the kitchen, Rob."

He came to an abrupt halt in the entrance of warm cinnamon scented room. Mac bumped into his back. "Why aren't any of you answering your phones?"

"You're dripping snow all over my hardwood floors." Luke held an unlit cigar between clenched teeth. The threesome, gathered around the wood block kitchen table, were playing cards. A solar lantern provided illumination, and a transistor radio gave an update about the electrical power restoration. "We're charging." He pointed toward the library. "Limited power from generator."

"And the landline?" Rob pointed to the wall phone.

Luke shrugged. "Didn't hear it."

"Mom!"

"Cassie!"

"What happened to your face?" Rob put his hand on his son's shoulder.

Marcus rubbed the side of his cheek and ear. "I had a misunderstanding with the princess and her pepper spray."

"I told you, I'm sorry." Cassie held her hands in the air, in surrender mode, then waved them. "I didn't totally trust him, and when he tried to assist me into the monster truck the spray went off, accidentally, and shot right onto his cheek and ear."

Although her face and form didn't resemble Mac;

her smile was an exact match.

"Hurt like hel—heck."

"The plan was for Luke to get her." Rob fisted his hands, trying to force his heart to slow. The clear image of the destruction at Mac's house caused his gut to clench and unclench.

"Too far away. I was closer. Besides we're fine, except for," Marcus pointed to his cheek, "red-hot swelling." He nodded to his father. "Time was of the essence is what you said, and of course, you taught me well."

Cassie tapped the back of his hand. "Doesn't detract from his handsomeness though."

A wide smile appeared on Marcus' bluish-pink mottled face. Rob shook his head. "Teenagers."

"Thank you, Marcus." Mac hugged him from the back. "I'm glad both of you are safe."

"Marcus, why don't you and Cassie get logs for the fireplace? Luke, how much fuel do you have for the generator?" The urgency and fear of immediate safety had passed. Foremost Rob planned to strategize.

"Enough to last throughout the night. If we don't have electricity tomorrow, we'll need to get supplies." Luke glanced between Rob and Mac.

After the two exuberant teens put their coats on and went outside with Scat trailing behind, Rob sat at the table. "We just came from Mac's house; someone hung a very lifelike plastic body from a rafter in the barn. He's a felon, a fan, an assaulter named Lee Snyder."

"Damn, no one's going to get our family. Where's my shotgun?" Luke vaulted from the chair.

"I hate to interrupt a testosterone moment, but I don't think he did it." Her narrow-eyed stare startled him. "By your owlish expression I can tell I need to explain. I hated the limelight and tried to put that chapter behind me. I relocated, and I'm using my real name, but the psycho found me anyway."

Rob's difficulty forming words was new and very annoying. "You don't think he hung the doll? He's the only one you have a protection order for, right?" He'd done his research and knew the answer; however, her response would determine their trust level.

A ping, ping, ping echoed in the noiseless kitchen. "It sounds as if you know the answer to that."

"Your impatience isn't going to help matters, son." Luke stilled Mac's hand, and the clinking stopped. "Who else would have reason to hang that in your barn?"

"I don't know. The detective told me they had a list of possible, ah, fanatics, but he didn't share the names." She put up her hand in the universal stop signal. "Before you say anything else, people who often appear in public attract crazies. According to the police, Snyder's not physically capable of murder, even pseudo-murder."

Rob paced, using his figure-eight thought processing pattern.

"Second, he trashed the house and left. He'd wait to see my reaction. Third, in a movie script I created a body had been found hanging in the bedroom. It was a message like the horse head in that thug movie. If Lee Snyder wanted to imitate the movie and to get the fear factor, he would hang a mannequin in the bedroom and not the barn. A pursuer knows every little detail about their prey. Snyder wants attention. A psychopath would hang a look-a-like, but not without some message stating, 'Look at what I've done. I did it for you." She rested her head on her hands. "Why though? I get the warning, like someone is coming for me. Who or what should I beware of?"

"That seems reasonable, but he's still a viable suspect. The sheriff will find him, and we'll get some answers." Complications surrounded her. She moved back to Indiana for the peace and contentment, now she has a trail of antagonists after her. Rob didn't know the detectives had a suspect list…it must be a note only and not in the data file. "As a follow-up on Luke's question, who else may want to warn you or harm you in some way?" What was it about her that kept him off balance?

"I can't imagine who'd dislike me enough to go to the trouble." She stood and paced.

He leaned against the doorframe, crossed his ankles and folded his arms. His keen instincts were telling him she was withholding information. "Cassie's father's family?"

"They've never made contact before, why would they initiate an interaction with a violent crime?" She sat, leaned against the chair back and put her palms on her knees.

"Ok. Let's start a list of random names. Throw out anything in past encounters that struck you as suspect." Luke removed a pad of paper and pen from one of the oak kitchen drawers. On the clean white paper, he divided the horizontal blue lines with a vertical line. On one side he wrote suspects and on the other side, ruled out. "First, since you're keeping a low profile, let's determine who knows you're living in Indiana."

"Friends, my agent, editor, after the football fundraiser everyone in Lantern."

"What about your parents?" Luke took a sip of coffee.

"They've passed away. As far as family, just a couple of distant aunts and neither would share my address with a random caller."

"Mac, I think you're a darling, but someone may not have had a positive reaction to your pleasant personality. Can you think of anyone you may have rubbed the wrong way?" Luke had his pen posed over the left column.

"No."

Rob shook his head. "Everyone who walks on earth has bumped into someone's ego at one point in time." He got two bottles of water from the fridge and gave one to her.

"I've had a few agitated encounters. We can rule out Rob." She smiled. "Let's see, your ex-girlfriend, Veronica Masters and Nick Black. A couple of Xavier's ex-boyfriends, they were all wrong for him, but I doubt they'd go to the effort. Maybe one percent of entertainment industry in LA because I insisted most of the Native American history remain truthful."

"What about Seattle? It appeared as if you shared something with him. He didn't seem very happy to see me arrive at the hotel." He hated that underlying roughness in his voice.

Mac stood, took a sip of water then gathered, and stacked dishes in the dishwasher. "Seattle's a friend. He's not a threat."

"What kind of friend?"

She pivoted, met his stare, then switched her gaze to the dishes. "Work friend."

Rob kept his face devoid of emotion, and hoped the jealousy eating away at him would retreat.

The boisterous teens entered, preventing further answers and questions. They deposited the wood in the box near the fireplace. "There are four sleeping bags in a cupboard in the garage, which we'll use them as beds for the night. Rob, go get them and I'll gather pillows." Luke winked at him. He knew.

****

Sleep evaded her. Travel, fear, threats, all created an adrenaline rush. A thump on the wood floor drew her attention. Scat lodged himself between her and Cassie's legs. She nudged him, and he comically shot four legs straight into the air. The fur between his paws was matted with dirty snow. She'd need to arrange grooming.

Rob's face appeared an inch away. The low embers of the fire created a faint glow, highlighting his sharp cheekbones. "Come with me."

He helped her rise from the hard floor. She tucked the covers around Cassie. Scat did not stir from his quick-onset slumber. His watchdog skills remained questionable.

Rob's large, calloused hand clasped hers as they tiptoed from the room. He gripped the kitchen doorknob. "I found out during my teenage years the kitchen door squeaks when it's three-fourths of the way closed. If I opened it slow at first and then fast at the end it didn't create an alarm for my parents."

"I can imagine you coming in after curfew and trying to be quiet. I bet you were a contrary teen."

He struck a match. Sulfur permeated the room. Candlelight dusted the silver hairs above his ears. The grays had progressed in the last few weeks, even more in the last two days.

"We need to talk." He slid onto a wood chair.

She sat on his lap. "I don't want to talk. I've pent up energy. In a time of crisis men and women turn to each other for comfort, for reassurance that life continues. It's a well-known fact more births happen nine months after a black out or disaster occurs." She kissed him. "Let's find someplace to comfort each other."

"There's nothing more I'd like than to help you expel energy—"

"Help me to forget the events from the last couple of days, just for a moment. I know for a fact you can create a heat which will last for hours." She slipped her hand under his flannel shirt.

His chuckle vibrated her palm.

"I'm glad you're hot." She burrowed.

"I'm going to take that as a multiple compliment."

"As it was intended."

"I care about you." He kissed her lightly. "I don't want you to get hurt."

"I care a great deal for you, too." She fused her lips with his and increased the force.

He detached. "Then tell me what you're hiding."

She sighed.

He leaned against the chairback. "I want a relationship based on trust. Trust must be two-way."

She nodded. "Trust is keeping your word to a person and is a direct reflection of character and integrity. Without honor, faith and belief, what is left of a person's character?"

"I understand you don't want to betray a confidence; however, in New York you said you wouldn't keep secrets."

"This secret was prior to the New York trip, so grandfathered secrets remain."

"You've a pact with Seattle?" He tapped his fingers on the table. "It's been a traumatic few days; however, above all else, I need you to trust me."

She wanted a relationship with this intense, intelligent man and as difficult as it would be, she needed to lean on someone, to have a solid foundation. "Aside from helping Caedmon, I'm assisting Seattle's tribe with a legal matter, which has no bearing on the current circumstances."

"You're in danger, and I've yet to determine who's the suspect." A muscle tick appeared on his jaw. "I'm not going to gamble with your life."

She pressed her fingertips along the outer ridge of his face. The roughness of his day-old beard prevented a smooth flow. The bristles made a sound like leaves blowing on top of each other in the wind. She ended the route by outlining his perfect lips. "I do trust you."

Chapter 16

Mac didn't use the "L" word freely. She hadn't been in a truly romantic relationship since Kurt. The emotional turmoil of her groom's death and abrupt awareness of how short life can be, altered her life forever. She entered the kitchen, inhaling the warm cinnamon laced air.

Rob poured coffee into a mug and the refreshing scent of brewed beans diminished the sluggish insomnious-ness.

"What did the police say when you talked to them last night?"

He jumped. The coffee tilted spilling molten liquid onto his thumb and onto the counter. "Damn." Rob set the container on the marble, snatched a towel off the sink and absorbed the brew dripping along the waterfall edge.

"Sorry. I thought you heard me come in. I've been told I have a hard walk." Mac rushed forward and plucked the cloth from his pinkening digit. "Here, let me. Do you have an ice pack?"

"Freezer door."

She removed a blue rectangle. The label had a crying child on the front, holding a cold pack to his skinned knee. She laughed. Luke had such a good sense of humor. "Sit down and put this on your hand."

Rob sat on the counter stool and applied the towel wrapped ice.

"Good, no blisters are forming." She looked into his eyes, noted the restlessness, the exhaustion.

"Shall I get you fresh cup?"

"Please and thank you."

"Are you hungry?"

"I could probably eat, if it were placed in front of me," he grumbled.

Her hand trembled as she placed a steaming cup of coffee on the table, then opened the refrigerator. "Eggs and bacon or pancakes?"

"Surprise me."

She set the oven's air fryer at 425 and spread strips of bacon on a cooking sheet, then popped them into the heat.

"The police were swamped with calls from a stranded motorist, older people and invalids who needed to be moved to the church, which serves as a temporary shelter during a crisis. Considering the situation, Chief Dawson promised to send an officer to your house directly. He also mentioned he would call or stop by if time permits, to get our statements."

"Have they found him?"

"Not yet. They did get a mugshot and current description. Last night I updated Luke about everything. He'll help to protect the kids."

"Thank you, Rob. I'm sorry you've been drawn into this madness." She removed bacon from the air fryer, and after plating, placed the crispy bites in front of him. "That's what relationships are all about, right?"

"Right." His lips brushed hers, making her feel as though the world would right itself.

A shaggy head popped around the corner. "Okay to enter?"

Mac jumped. "Sure."

Luke chuckled and entered the kitchen followed by Marcus and Cassie.

Mac dredged up some air. "I'll scramble eggs if someone will take Scat outside to do his business."

"Come on Cassie, we'll take him out." Marcus nudged her arm.

Within a few minutes barking and laughter filtered from the exterior.

"This is terrific coffee, Luke." Mac shut the entrance door.

"Only the best." He poured a cup and added two teaspoons of sugar and a touch of cream, then inhaled. "Yep, good stuff."

She broke eggs into a blue and brown ceramic bowl. "Do you hear a doorbell?"

"I'll get it." Luke strolled from the kitchen, an empty cup dangling from his fingers.

The teens returned with a wet dog in tow, who placed his nose near the bacon. Rob moved the platter, precariously close to the edge, to the center.

Scat gripped the counter with his front paws.

"Down, Scat," Rob said. The dog sat on the floor; drool ran in slobbery strands from the sides of his jaws to pool between his feet.

"Mac, I'd like for you and Cassie to join Marcus and me at a resort in Georgia over spring vacation." Rob lifted his mug.

"My pref is Miami Beach. Could you teach me to salsa dance, Cassie?" Marcus asked and removed orange juice and carton of milk from the fridge. Several seconds passed. "Cassie?"

"What?" Her surly tone punctured the room.

Not intimidated by her cutting, raised voice, the brave lad continued, "When's your spring break?"

She shoved her plate forward and crossed her arms at her waist. "I'm on break now. I finished earlier, so I could spend some alone time with my mother in freekin Indiana."

"Cassie, Marcus and I don't want to interrupt your time with Mac, if you would rather not go."

"This group trip is rather sudden don't you think?" Cassie replied. "May I talk to you alone, Mother?"

Appalled by her daughter's behavior, she exhaled. "If you'll excuse us. Cassie, let's talk in private."

They walked toward the library. A man stood in the foyer. His khaki and brown uniform was highlighted by a silver badge reflecting light from the transom window. "Luke."

Cassie halted. "I need to get my phone."

Luke shut the door and nodded a greeting. "Melvin, how are you this early morning?"

Melvin gave him a thumbs up. "Uh, has Rob left yet? I need to get a statement from him and uh," he removed a notebook from a pocket, "McCartney James."

"Sure, I'll show you to the kitchen."

Mac and Cassie paused in the hallway. "Mac, this is Deputy Madson, and he's here to take your statement."

"Hello, this is my daughter, Cassandra." Mac extended her hand.

He held onto her hand longer than protocol. She gave a quick shake and shoved her digits into her pocket. "Your name is Me—"

"Call me Jake. I'm Deputy Melvin Jacob Madson, but I'd prefer Jake. I'm here to marry you." His baritone voice didn't leave room for argument.

She took a step back. Luke covered a laugh with a cough. Mac glared at him.

"Oops. I mean, take your statement." Flustered, he inhaled, and his cheeks flushed crimson. He pursed his lips and nodded toward Cassie. "Hi. Nice to meet you." After a long exhale, he rubbed his earlobe. "I'm sorry. I'm a fan and here you are, in the flesh."

Luke laughed. "Looks like you bagged another one."

"Stop." Mac pivoted, going in the direction of the east hallway. "Rob's in the kitchen. Could you get his statement first, while I talk to my daughter for a few minutes?"

"Sure, sure. I look forward to spending time with you. Rather take your statement." He strutted toward the kitchen.

Mac waved her hand, creating a slight breeze. "It's like an oven in here."

"Yeah, the electricity's on." Cassie grabbed her cellphone, and they walked to the library. Cassie plopped onto the brown leather sofa.

"I can't wait to take a hot shower." Mac smiled and sat on the edge of the couch.

"Why didn't you tell me about Rob?" Cassie coiled her reddish-brown hair into a ponytail. With her rail-thin dancer's body and no makeup she looked like she was twelve years old. However, the anger radiating from her voice and stiff shoulders made her resemble a hellcat.

"I planned to tell you, when I saw you in New York. Then I found out you came here. You're my focus. Until I knew you were safe nothing else mattered. I never want to experience that horrible fear again."

"I forgot you were coming to New York. Riley and

I broke up. He left me. I wanted to be with you. I needed you." She ran her index finger around in circles on the leather arm of the chair. "You said you'd always be there for me."

Mac scooted closer. "I know, baby. When Katlin told me about you and Riley, I wanted to be with you, too." She put her arm around Cassie and held her close. It was easy to forget inside this young woman's body existed a little girl, with little girl fears. "Tell me about it."

"He wanted more than I wanted to give, I guess. I'm not ready for the whole intimacy thing. Maybe in part because I never saw you have an intimate relationship, until now. Are you over my father then?"

"Your father and I shared a timeless love, but the accident took him away from us. He's been gone for over eighteen years." Mac paused, contemplating how to discuss Rob.

"I'm not sure what to think. I've never seen you so close to someone, and he kissed you in front of me. You walk around the room, and he watches you. His eyes are all, I don't know, soft. I guess I'm jealous, because I thought you'd always be committed to me and my father."

Mac held her gaze. "Honey, I loved your father so very much. I wish you could've known him. He was amazing: humorous, sensitive, and loving. I never imagined finding someone I'd want to share my life with again." She grimaced. Should she feel guilty? No, Cassie was a young adult, having experienced love and heartache. "I think I'm falling in love with Rob."

"Mom, I'm sorry. You deserve to have someone care about you. It just threw me when I thought you'd be there, and you weren't. You're always there." Sadness flooded her face. "Especially since you live here, and I'm in New York."

She laid her cheek on top of her daughter's head and stroked her hair. "Sweetheart, I'll always be there for you. I thought you liked Lantern and the house. This is the second time you brought up the move. When we came here and stayed for a couple of weeks you said it would be great for me to live here and compared the cottage to visiting your grandparents' farm. What happened between then and now?"

"I didn't realize how much I'd miss you and how much I still need you. You've found someone else to love." Cassie sounded like a petulant child.

"I've found a connection with Rob. This thing we share wasn't by design, just instant." She exhaled. "I'm still adjusting to our relationship." She tipped Cassie's face up to make direct eye contact. "I have enough love for you, Rob, Marcus, Luke, and even Scat, but I'll only have one daughter."

"I think Rob's in love with you, too," Cassie whispered.

"Hey, Dad sent me to tell you Jake must leave, so could you give your statement now?" Marcus looked between the two women. "Also, Grandpa wants to know if Cassie could go with us to take care of the horses. He said to tell you he'll carry a firearm."

"I don't think so, Marcus. I want to keep her close until Snyder has been found."

"Mom, I'll be okay. I promise I'll always be with Marcus or Luke. I won't go off by myself. Please! I love horses." Her deep brown eyes glimmered.

"I don't think that's a good idea."

"I'll protect her." Marcus' deep voice personified solemness and sincerity. A sudden new maturity changed his lean face. Other than the snapping wood in the fireplace the room was quiet, his vow resounded in the silence.

"I trust you, Marcus. I'll put my only daughter in your hands." She hugged her, then wiped away the pooled tears. "Wear warm clothes you two, its cold outside."

"So, are we going to Georgia or what?" Marcus held out his youthful fingers.

"I guess I'll be able to stand your ugly mug for a couple of weeks." Cassie accepted his hand and gracefully rose from the sofa.

"Ah, she loves me already."

Mac chuckled as she entered the kitchen. "Please keep them close to you, Luke. I know I can trust you, but there's a crazy out there, and I don't want him to attack the people I love."

"Don't worry. I've the trusty 35 right here." He slapped his side holster. "No one's going to get near either of those kids. I'll take the ugly dog with us, too." Luke sauntered through the hallway.

"I'm sorry to rush you, but I need to return to the station. If you'd rather, I could come to your house later." A wide smile spread across the deputy's face.

"Her statement will be the same as mine, and now's a good time." Rob's sharp tone erased Jake's smile.

Mac sent him a quick surprised look, then refilled her coffee cup. She sat beside Rob and covered his hand with hers. "We were together, just returned from New York, when we found the damage. Our statements will be identical."

Jake swallowed, making his Adam's apple lift and lower. "I see, together."

"Yes, together." She braided her fingers with Robs.

"I see. Well, you'll need to give your version on a statement." Jake's face infused with color as he shuffled papers.

She recited the discovery of the house and then the mannequin. "Please let me know when to come to the station and sign." She stood. "Thank you."

"Sure, I'll let you know." Jake glanced at Rob. "So, is Veronica free?"

"Buddy, she's all yours. Any word on Snyder?"

"Not yet. We've put out an APB, an inquiry. We've a lead, although the weather will delay things a bit." Jake put on his overcoat, stuffed his notebook into a pocket and marched toward the door. "Thanks for your hospitality. Ms. James, it's a pleasure meeting you. I've seen your documentaries. I can't wait for Red Hot to be released."

"Thank you." Mac smiled at Rob. "Excuse me, please." She ran up the stairs. After showering she dressed in the same blue jeans, a dark green cashmere turtleneck sweater and half boots. Wet hair twisted and secured, she searched her handbag then applied the essentials, eyeliner and lip gloss.

"Today, we'll go to your house to review your security footage, or do you have a link on your phone?" He placed his hands on her waist. She turned wrapped her arms around his neck, kissed the soft skin and inhaled his scent. A simple clove and spice bay rum aroma, she'd used a similar soap in the shower earlier.

"Back away from the woman." The gruff voice vibrated through the room.

Chapter 17

"I like porn as much, if not more than the next fella but we need to get goin'. Let go of the bitch. Now." His blunt tone sounded like one of guys from the gangster soap opera Seattle had playing on the TV in New York. The man had a nasal voice pitch, certainly from a linguistics perspective he was from the New Jersey area.

Rob released her and pivoted. Mac peered over his shoulder to get a visual. Two men. Her breath caught. They looked like criminals.

Rob pushed her behind him and threw a punch, hitting the bigger of the two. At the same time the shorter guy used a metal object and hit the side of Rob's head. He fell like a solid walnut tree. Blood seeped from his temple. She threw herself on top, shielding him from other blows.

A heavy hand grasped her arm. Jerked backward, he dragged her across the floor, scraping her fingers on the wood surface. Her fingernails snapped with each attempt to grip whatever would give her leverage.

"Nick, stand her up. We need to jet."

He firmly grasped her arm and catapulted her upward. She scrambled, trying to remember Xavier's self-defense lessons. She lifted her leg and roundhouse kick-boxed Nick. Her foot landed flat on the right side of his face, leaving a boot shaped welt.

With a brief glance at porn guy, she ran. His smirk

should have been a warning. His fat fist slammed into her left cheek. She tried to shake it off, but darkness took over.

A tight blindfold prevented Mac from opening her eyes. Hot pounding pain radiated through her head. She moved her shoulders. Bound by zip ties, sharp tingling jolts raced through her wrists. Touching her face with the inner skin of her upper arm, she used the torn cloth to wipe away moisture. The motor of a vehicle roared as the driver shifted gears.

"Joe, I need ice for my face. The bitch left an imprint of a God-damn heel. I'm God-damn branded." Nick's whiny voice sounded like a five-year-old in a tantrum.

"Can't. The boss expects us in thirty minutes." Porn guy's name was Joe. Their chatter covered her movements as she dug her heels into the seat. She scooted to the right and bumped into a hard cushion.

"There, Joe. A VP. Quick in and out."

"Okay. The store is monitored, so don't swipe the bag, pay the damn dollar fifty for it." His flat-out voice tone did not disguise his frustration. They had a schedule. Why was time an element? Who's the boss? Was Rob alive?

The vehicle came to a hasty halt. She rolled and shoved her feet against a hard surface to prevent falling. A click and a squeak, then the rustle of cloth indicated someone, probably Nick, exited. Chilled air rolled across her face.

She mentally assessed her plight. Her senses compensated, no sight but acute hearing. Fetid air infiltrated the space, until a fresh breeze entered again. She forced her legs, shoulders and neck to relax. *Focus. Focus. Focus.*

She expected one of them to discover her unconscious ruse and jab her. Joe didn't immediately move, just loudly exhaled a noxious garlic odor.

Her lower body wasn't bound by plastic ties, which was odd considering she used her leg to clock Nick. Luke and the kids should have returned by now. They would find Rob and get him medical help. He'd survive.

****

Rob recognized the voice but couldn't quite make a connection. His back, at a ninety-degree angle, enabled him to lean on an elbow. He closed his eyes, trying to keep the pain out and the nausea controlled. Lights flashed, and the blinding agony made vomit rise to his throat. He lowered himself flat to the floor, tightly closed his eyes, and concentrated on keeping the bile contained. His salvia glands secreted a glaze to pave the way for the vile fluid to erupt. He swallowed. Heavy footsteps pounded on the hardwood floor, running water, then thumping again. Wait. Attack. Fight.

"Here, drink this." Seattle Coyote. His strong-arm propelled Rob forward. "Drink. Only a sip." His annoying persistent voice came through loud and clear, like the gong of Sunday church bells.

Rob lifted his arm to tip the glass, and the cold water dripped into his mouth, cooling his throat as it washed the puke. The memories flooded back in those few seconds. "I need to go. Mac. They've taken her."

The pain behind his eyes was excruciating. He touched the sore area; blood came away on his index finger.

"The wise guys?" Seattle asked.

Rob opened his eyes a mere slit "Help me up."

"You've a cut on your head, probably will need

stitches. Give me details, and I'll track her while you get medical attention." Seattle helped him to stand.

The wooziness slowly dissipated, but unsteady on his feet, he grabbed the counter and crept toward the sink.

"No time for stitches. The cabinet, on the end, has supplies bandages and stuff inside a kit." Rob kept his eyes closed, blocking the light helped a little.

Coyote rustled around in the cabinet, then slammed it shut. "This one?"

Rob opened his eyes. "Yes. Hand me several pain relievers."

Seattle shoved a few white pills into his hand.

Rob tossed them into his mouth and chewed. With a flick of his wrist, he thrust a few into his pants pocket. He flipped on the faucet and scooped water into his mouth, washing the chalky residue past his throat. He diverted lukewarm water over his head, creating an unbearable sting. When the stream became pink, he stopped the torture, grabbed a towel and applied pressure to the wound. As a former Beret he'd suffered worse. "Let's go."

He glanced at Seattle. "In the long door to the right of the refrigerator is a pantry, grab a couple of gallons of water and the rifle in the mudroom."

Rob plucked a coat and hat off the rack, forced his feet into his boots, then snagged a hunting knife from the trophy display. Seattle followed him outside, carrying a large canvas bag.

Rob turned a one-eighty in the recently plowed snow and swallowed vomit. "Where's my truck?"

"It wasn't here when I arrived. The back door had been left open and banged against the side of the house.

An obvious clue, if you wondered why I was in your father's house, uninvited." Seattle tipped his black hat farther onto his head.

"I'm thankful you came by. What wise guys?" The fog lifted. He contemplated calling for back-up.

Seattle opened the passenger door. "Get in."

Rob plopped onto the seat. Seattle handed him the first-aid kit and tossed the equipment onto the backseat.

Rob set the box on his lap, found butterfly bindings, then flipped the vanity mirror to affix the bandages. He threw the box onto the backseat and removed his cellphone from his jean's pocket. He pressed Marcus' link.

"Hey, what's up?" Marcus's bright, happy, voice transmitted across the line. Sweet relief overwhelmed Rob, his son was safe.

"Is Luke with you?" His voice came out as husky as the dry stalks of corn in November.

"Yes, he's right here."

After a bit of rustling, Luke said, "Hi, Rob."

"A couple of men came into your house and took Mac. Seattle Coyote and I are on their trail. For safety, I'd like for all of you to remain at my house."

"I'll help," Luke stated with the force of a man who wouldn't be reckoned with and the grit of a male protecting a loved one.

"You will. Keep the kids safe. It'll be less of a worry for us."

"Ok. I'll keep them in the house. Your manager has everything under control." Luke paused and silence filtered through the connection. "Rob, be careful."

"We will." A peace settled over him. The wall erected four years ago, crumbled inch by inch. All because of circumstances centering around one woman who'd turned his life topsy-turvy.

Rob peered out the car window. They were headed toward the village. He punched a sequence of numbers and hit speaker.

"Deputy Madson, Lantern Police Department."

"Jake, it's Rob. A couple of guys broke into my father's house right after you left. They kidnapped Mac."

"Wasn't Lee Snyder, we picked him up a few minutes ago. Did you get a look at the kidnappers?" Jake's loud voice echoed through the car.

"One wore a cap, shielding his brow and shaded his eyes. Both men wore dark suits, and the taller man had on a duster. It caught my eye as I went down. Out of place in Lantern."

"It's been forty-five minutes," Seattle said. "Two men. Brown hair, one was five foot seven and one was five-five. The shorter guy had close-set brown eyes and talked with an Italian accent." He paused. "Probably from New Jersey."

"Other than their clothing and accents is there anything else distinguishable, which would set them apart?"

"Sorry, not enough time." The information provided was sufficient to arrest suspects, but a small town didn't have a lot of criminals invading. Rob coughed. "They caught us at an awkward moment." Seattle's screwed facial expression told him more than words. But he was still going to ask the questions that plagued him.

"We'll find her. I'll send a deputy over to Luke's house to try and get fingerprints. Was there a scuffle?"

"Seattle?" Rob held the device in his direction.

"Nothing seemed to be disturbed, either she went

without an argument, or they put everything back. My money's on, they put everything back." His flat monotone voice grew harsh.

"She'd fight," Rob insisted. A thrill ran through him, knowing she'd battle, then alarm chased the moment.

"I'll keep in contact."

"Thanks." He disconnected and stared at Seattle.

"I know that you're a fan of crime shows, but you didn't see or hear them, right?" He was suspicious of Seattle's assurance the men were from the only location he wanted to visit in the garden state.

"I was at Mac's house and saw two men who fit the description you gave to Jake. They didn't realize their voices carried through the woods, especially with the snow as a sounding board. Italian accents. They were looking for her."

"Did they say why they wanted her?"

"No, just disappointed she wasn't there. Somehow, they knew Luke's name. I went to your father's house." Seattle took his glance off the road and faced Rob. "You know the rest of the story."

Rob turned in the seat. "Mac is honorable. She would not betray your secret; although, the truth about what you two have been hiding for the past few months might help us find her." The hard edge on each word should have unnerved the man. Seattle didn't flinch; the answer would not be what he wanted to hear.

"I cannot betray my tribe," Seattle softly replied.

"Do you love her?" Rob croaked out.

"I have an affection for her." Seattle's jaws clamped and a muscle tick formed in his right cheek.

His heart sped, and his breath caught. Would he have the same issue he'd had with his wife? "Are you having an affair with her?"

Seattle stopped the car at a crossroads and met Rob's stare. "No. She's in love with you. If you don't love her, I'd like to know."

"I do. Tell me what's going on." Rob slowly drew out the hunting knife and held it along his thigh. If it came down to threatening his friend to save Mac, so be it. "What game are you playing?"

"Game! You should know Mac well enough by now to realize she doesn't play games. She embraces life with gusto. Honesty is part of her DNA. Although, I'm not a fan of her saying whatever she thinks." He paused. "Most of the time, I wish she'd filter her thoughts."

"Doesn't explain why two Jersey men kidnapped her?" He unsnapped his seatbelt.

"She helped Caedmon prepare for law exams. He's going to help us get a patent. The secret the council asked her to keep concerns a fuel alternative. Native Americans have been cheated since the first white man landed on our soil. We'll not let this innovative product be stolen."

"You developed a fuel alternative using what products?"

"The formula allows a combination of plant, mineral and water to create a fuel source comparable to petrol. It's inexpensive to make and will save the environment from the toxic chemicals produced by gasoline waste."

Rob replaced the knife into the depths of his pocket. "Since we're driving to the village a greedy someone from the tribe is planning to steal the product."

"It appears to be true." Seattle drove through the crossroads.

"Who are the suspects?"

"A girl I've been with."

"Ah. Jealousy is a key force behind most violent crimes." He hoped the betrayal was a simple case of jealousy and not greed. Greed and jealousy were a lethal combination.

"What's your plan?"

"I'll talk to Jennifer. If needed, I'll call in the council. Hopefully, it's a matter of trust, and we'll resolve the issue."

"Why take Mac? Wouldn't Caedmon or you be a more logical choice?"

"I'm not sure."

"The resolution won't be as uncomplicated as talking to a woman. Especially a possessive woman."

"Yep."

Trees, pines, ancient oaks created a thick green and brown forest of the eighty-eight-acre tract being used as a Natural Area for botanical research. Rob wasn't surprised they'd created a formula using natural ingredients.

Seattle stopped the car in front of a dung brown cabin. The shutters hung lopsided, and a faint cheerless light appeared inside. Billows of smoke spewed from the chimney. Rob swung the door open before the car completely stopped.

"I'd appreciate it, if you'd let me do this alone," Seattle growled.

"No. My woman's missing. I want to hear what yours has to say." Rob stood, steadied, then walked around to the front of the car.

Seattle grabbed his arm. "It's private. I'm sure you'll respect that."

He glanced at the gloved fingers gripping his arm. The hand of an honorable man who'd assisted him earlier.

"I'll wait here. If she doesn't provide you with the answers, you won't need to call in the council." The only viable link to the men who took Mac was inside that house. He'd get answers. He leaned against the front fender and prayed his headache would fade.

The sun was mostly wrapped around a cluster of pine trees, barely moving twenty minutes later when Seattle reappeared. "Jennifer volunteered to watch Mac when Snyder arrived. She didn't warn Mac or tell the council members. We need to find her father, he's responsible."

Rob rushed toward the woman on the porch. Seattle ran forward and held his arm.

"No, for a man of intelligence you are letting your emotions rule. We have a bigger issue at hand." Seattle climbed in the car and slammed the door.

He'd never let his emotions interfere with a mission; however, Mac wasn't just a job. Seated in the car, he asked, "Where do we find the father?"

"Philippe can be found at the local gathering hut. He hired guys from a place called Little Chicago." He drove east.

Rob glanced at the woman. Her hands covered her face, and her shoulders shook. He didn't feel sorry for her. She'd created her own misery.

He pictured a hut, where people sat around a fire smoking a peace pipe; however, the block style building had cedar siding and a tin roof. A porch ran the entire length, adding support for the overhang. Logs, solid tree trunks with the bark still attached in some places added to the rustic façade. The clean lines of the old fashion rocking chairs, with their bent wood structure, remained intact despite the snow covering the outer edges.

The gust of heat from the wood burning stove and the smell of tobacco, cigars and cigarettes, overloaded his senses. It didn't take long to pinpoint his prey. Anticipation made his muscles tense. Rob greeted everyone, as his property butted up against the sacrosanct land, so he knew most of the villagers.

"Philippe, I'd like to talk to you in private." Seattle's stiff walk and unyielding stance added power to his words. He impatiently jingled the keys clutched in his hand. A less timid man would have crawled into a corner and indeed Philippe glanced at the exit. The men at the table stopped talking.

"I've been looking for you. For those of you who do not know him, this is Seattle Coyote, my future son-in-law." Philippe slurred the words and grabbed a beer. "Cheers."

A round of congratulations went through the crowd. Seattle leaned, bumping his chest into the short dark man. "Let's go outside."

Philippe gave a half-hearted chuckle and put his amber glass bottle on the table. He snatched a coat from a chair and covered his torn brown flannel shirt. "Nervous groom."

The men mumbled greetings. Once outside, Philippe ran. Faster, younger and not inebriated, Rob grabbed him by the scruff of his neck. "You had the scum bags take my fiancée. I want to know where she's at, or you and I are walking into the woods a few feet away and only one of us is returning."

"You talk crazy man." Philippe glanced at Seattle. "Seattle, jump in here. I'm going to be your father-in-law." The cool temperature did not prevent the sweat from rolling along his whiskered cheeks.

"Tell us what you know old man," Seattle demanded.

"I don't know her, and I don't know anything. If your girlfriend's missing maybe she found a man to attend her, like your first wife did." Philippe licked his lips.

Rob drew back his fist, craving to strike that square face. With lightning quick action Seattle stopped his hand, preventing the snap.

"If you hit him, he'll be out cold, and our trail will be lost."

He considered the situation, nodded and stepped back. Seattle withdrew a switchblade from his left boot, flicked it open and held the shiny pinpoint to the weasel's jugular vein.

"Seattle," Philippe begged. His Adam's apple bobbed. The small man's sweat mingled with the stench of putrid beer.

"Jennifer told me everything. You'll provide names and locations" Seattle nicked the vile creature's neck, drawing a pinpoint of blood. "Or your alcohol-laced body fluid will flood the ground."

Other than Philippe's sharp intake of breath, a coyote's mournful howling echoed in the distance. Seattle added pressure to the knife, slicing through the skin.

"She told you about Liza?" Philippe squeaked.

"Yes, and about your part in Mac's abduction," Seattle said. "Rob, untie and remove his socks and boots."

Philippe tightened his lips. "She's been taken to the hermit's cabin near Pioneer Pass. She'll die if you do not arrive, alone, at midnight."

Rob removed the man's well-worn boots and thin socks. "It's six o'clock now." He wished he could do real physical damage to his drunk, instead he stood. "What do they want?"

Seattle knelt in front of Philippe and held a hunting knife over the great toe of his right foot.

"How many are there?" Rob insisted.

"I don't know."

"Your cold feet will not get numb, because I want you to feel each cut to the digits. Last chance, how many?" Seattle Coyote, the beast of the night had been released from his personal strictures of society.

With quick panted cloud puffs of air Philippe gasped, then shook his head.

"Wasting time. We need to go." Rob looked toward the frosted foothills, and prayed she was unharmed. Leakage seeped onto his forehead. He touched the bandage, and it slid. Damn, he'd need to wrap a bandana around his head to keep the gore contained.

Seattle inserted the knife, digging into the toe skin. "Two or three?"

"There are two men. Too intense, she concentrated on the project from a distance," Philippe answered as a thin red line of plasma seeped into the ground. "They'll trade her for the chemical recipe."

Seattle wiped his knife on a boulder. "We'll bind him and stuff him into the trunk. The jail is enroute, so we'll drop him off. It's a three-to-four-hour trek to the hermit's cabin by car, but with horses we'll get there in less than two."

"Great. Let's go. Call the law and without stopping we'll roll him onto the ground outside the building."

Chapter 18

Rob's horse ambled off the path, hugging the branches of the Blue Spruce trees. Buckets of snow dropped from the limbs and coated his right leg. "Whoa." He ran his hand under the thick mane of his horse, trying to relax the gelding without disrupting the LED attached to the leather halter. "A considerable amount of time has passed since you traveled this route. Are you sure you remember the way to the house? Especially in the dark."

"Yes. On the brink of manhood an adolescent male spends three days with a knife and string near the cabin." Seattle choked on the words. "It's been years, but I know the area well."

"The she Picatelli mentioned is Liza Carpenter? They are having an affair?" He shuddered at the thought of the two of them together. Picatelli, a drunken slob and Liza was a small mean woman with brittle hair and a sharp tongue, a combination not worth thought time.

"Yes."

"Do you trust Picatelli, when he said you need to go in alone?" Rob pulled on the left rein. His brown-speckled horse may have vision problems, which would provide a logical reason for it to veer to the right, or he simply wanted to walk under the trees. Appaloosas had their own mind set and this horse certainly did what he wanted. Leather creaked as he resituated himself on the saddle. The surrounding woods were silent except for the continual yip howls of the coyotes. A full moon played hide-and-seek behind the clouds. Damn, he could not get a break today.

"Picatelli is a liar. Half of what he says is fiction."

"You know the layout of the cabin and the land. Give me details, I want to go prepared."

Seattle straightened his shoulders. "When did you and Mac become engaged?"

"It's not official. I assume there's a back door?"

"The cabin's little more than a shack. One door, two windows, faces the barn. South, behind the barn, is Leak Creek, slow running and this time of the year the stream will be frozen."

To avoid being bitten, Rob tugged the horse's reins. The path narrowed, so he tagged behind Seattle.

"We're traveling east and toward the mountains. West will take you to Pioneer Lost. It's a strip of low-lying ground that's generally wet all summer long. When the pioneers first cut through, many animals and one woman were lost in the maze of a swamp-like area." Seattle shifted in his seat.

"Okay. Not west," Rob replied. He refused to be a victim of the maze, and he wasn't leaving without her.

"I'll go in alone. We've the advantage and…"

"And?" Rob's training equipped him to take on three men but going alone might put Mac in danger.

"I'll insist we go to the barn. I'll write out the formula and suggest creating a sample, which will give us additional time."

"They will require you to mix the formula and check the accuracy. Then they will kill you and Mac once it's validated. Assuming there are only two, they'll divide. I'll go into the shack and get her."

"Yes, then leave. With your skill set you'll get her to safety."

Rob used his teeth to remove a glove and extracted a couple of pain killers from his pocket. He popped the aspirin, chewed and swallowed. "Thankfully, it's not snowing. We need surveillance first."

****

They tied their horses a good distance from the shack. Seattle pointed to a hunter's deer stand in the trees. The wooden structure, five or six pieces of wood braced with old bug-ridden two-by-fours was held together by the act of nature. They climbed the icy ladder and scouted the area. A fragile light filtered from uncovered dirty windows. Parked near a ramshackle barn, an older version black town car had a dusting of snow, so they'd been there for a couple of hours.

Rob evaluated the set up. Light escaped through the cracks of the structure, located ten feet from the cabin. One sliding door faced the shack, and minuscule air vents were on both sides.

The shack door opened. Wind caught the panel, thrusting it against the wall with a thunderous clap. A gleam of light provided the outline of a man. He slammed the door, and with a short stiff walk trudged through the powder. He lifted the trunk lid and removed a few large canvas bags. He struggled to carry the drooping duffels into the barn.

"I think we should go in now," Seattle whispered.

Rob laid the rifle down. "No, not yet. We haven't seen her. There could be more than two. Midnight was the deadline." He raised the sleeve of his coat. The numbers shined bright green on his watch. "Eleven-thirty, we've time."

"I'm going behind the cabin. Send a warning, an owl's hoot; otherwise, I'm going in at midnight." Seattle nimbly descended the ladder and disappeared into the dense forest.

He wanted to storm the shack, but that was all emotion. Luke taught him patience. Get as much information as possible, come to a logical decision and then act. This tactic paid off during his military career, and it would today.

The man exited the barn and shut the car's trunk. A branch from a nearby tree broke and like falling on stairsteps clanked its way to the ground with a soft thud, a damn two feet from his perch. Aware of the noise, the kidnapper cocked his head to the left.

Rob flatted himself on the surface of the platform, banging his head on a post. Seattle blended with the side of the shack. "Hoot!"

Stocky man reached into his coat: sliver glints, of a gun, flashed in the limited light. Rob gripped the rifle and scurried down the ladder. Shielded by walnut trees he screeched, "Hoot!"

A gunshot split the air, and a whizzing bullet embedded in the bark. Steam engine gasps of air hurt his aspirin coated throat as he ran from tree to tree. He pressed his back against the shack wall. No visual of Seattle.

At the wall's edge, he held onto the corner and peered around. No sign of life. He licked a drip of salty condensation from his lip.

Murmured voices came from inside the shack. The cabin windows provided a faint glimmer of light. A crackle of branches drew his attention. He squatted and pointed the rifle in the direction of the noise.

"Don't shoot." The voice, as faint as leaves blowing through the air, made him furious.

"Dad?" Rob hissed, mirroring his disbelief and displeasure.

"Come," Luke insisted.

Rob lowered his gun and walked toward the edge of the cabin, checked all directions and trudged across the clearing to a sheltering tree. He slipped behind the massive trunk of a maple and glanced around.

"Here, son." His father stood near the next tree dressed in Eskimo garb. The dark anorak coat, complete with fur around the edges, outerwear pants, boots and protective gloves blended with the night. He flicked his fingers.

Rob followed him until they came to a natural alcove twenty feet from the shack. The slice of a recess, no bigger than a water trough, made entering a challenge. Luke clicked on a pen light, providing a bit of illumination in the dark interior.

Branches scratched their outwear as they crept further into the opening. At six-foot-five, he didn't have to lean, the bower felt large and airy.

"Why aren't you protecting the kids?" Bolts of anger flew from his cold lips.

"Dr. Worth and Xavier, Cassie's godfather, are with them. Unable to reach anyone they showed up at your house. Now, how do we proceed?"

Rob scratched a cobweb from his chin. "You don't do anything."

"Son, it's clear you're alone. Seattle's been abducted?" Luke's rebuttal came out as razor-sharp as a steel tracker.

"My responsibility." Rob bent his knees to crawl

from the pine shielded grotto.

"She lied to both of us." The rigid words bounced of the secret-keeping natural walls.

Rob froze, then did an about face.

"I want the bad blood aired now, before we go into a serious battle with guns. And I'm telling you Robert, I'll be going in." Luke leveled the filtered light near his chin, creating a halo around his face.

"Okay, Luke. We don't have much time, so say your peace and God willing, we'll both come out of this alive." He was weary from the strife and anxious to make a move. His head hurt like a bunch of banshees had settled in for the night.

"I understand time is of the essence, so I'll jump right to the point. I don't mean to speak ill of the dead, but your past wife was a lying cheat of a woman. She came to me to ask for money, so that she could buy the two of you a vacation package for a romantic anniversary getaway. Surprise trip, she said. Needed additional funds the next week, then a few days later she declared the price of the airfare had gone up, and she wanted more greenbacks. We went to lunch, where you saw us together. I planned to go to the travel agent and demand the initial price, the one agreed upon. She didn't want you to be suspicious, so I willingly handed her the cash with the belief that you were going to get an escape, the ride of your life." Luke sighed.

Rob unclamped his tight jaws. "The outcome could've been different if you'd told me."

"I've wanted to tell you what a fool I'd been to trust her. I knew her history, how unfaithful she'd been to you. Her drug problem. She said she'd changed. I gave her the money and in essence I killed her." Luke lowered the light. "You have every right to blame me."

His anger receded. "I wish you would've discussed this with me before today."

"I tried, but you wouldn't bend, stubborn like your old man. I blamed myself. If I couldn't forgive myself, why should I expect you to forgive me?" The hoarseness in his voice, the sadness of the lost years spurred Rob.

He nodded, then released a four-year-long awaited sigh. "Forgive yourself. Now, let's get Mac and Seattle. I'll go to the barn, where Seattle is being held. You go to the cabin, look in the windows, get the layout and number of people inside. Don't take any chances. I'll release Seattle, then all of us will get Mac."

Snap click resounded as his father slid his shotgun into the scabbard holster.

Chapter 19

Mac, scared, no, terrified more than she thought possible, crossed her legs. "I need to use the restroom. Could we stop, please?"

"Hold it. We only have ten minutes, before we get there."

"Ten minutes until we arrive where?"

"You're blindfolded for a reason, bitch. Shut up," Joe snapped.

Each bump added pressure to her already over-loaded bladder. She tried to mentally retreat to her favorite vacation spot, the ocean. The visualization worked until the waves reminded her of the need to urinate. She shifted her thoughts to the peacefulness of the back porch of her little cottage. The warm bubbling waters of the hot springs made her bladder cramp.

When had she last updated her will?

The abrupt stop propelled her sideways and onto the floor. The backdoor opened and a wave of hail assaulted her. She attempted to maneuver in the confined space. If she could stabilize, perhaps she could kick. A slimy paw grabbed her bound wrists and jerked her from the car.

"Ouch. You're bruising my back." Forced upright she was propelled forward.

"Up the stairs now."

She stumbled on three treads and tripped over the threshold of a doorway. Bitter cold metal was inserted between her face and the blindfold. She inhaled expecting to die, instead the knife cleanly sliced the binding. Tendrils of brutally cut hair floated to the floor. The numbness left and heat radiated through her freed hands.

"Facilities?"

"Toilet is outside Miss hoity-toity, or there's a bucket in the corner." He pointed toward a rusted can.

She pivoted. "I'll go outside, alone."

"No. You use the can."

Mac shuffled to the corner. The can's dirty label in addition to the strong waste scent made her shudder. Two-fingered she gripped the can and rushed into the only room with a less than complete door, lifted her jacket, lowered her slacks and hovered. The rush of urine provided instant relief. Trousers resituated, she searched the room for a weapon, anything to use for self-defense.

The rotting door flew open. She chucked the container of warm pee. Joe, because there wasn't an imprint of a boot on his face, ducked and attacked her, knocking her to the floor. She twisted and bucked, shifting his balance but not enough to dislodge him. He wrapped a hand around her throat and squeezed. Her breath came out shallow and harsh. She ran the sharp edges of her recently snapped off nails along his cheek.

He grabbed her wrists and held them above her head. "Bitch."

On top of her, he ground his erection between her thighs. She writhed and pressed her fingers into his palms.

A gunshot sounded outside the room, followed by a thud and a curse. Joe turned toward the noise, providing her an opportunity. She smashed her forehead directly onto his chin.

"Bitch." He sprang upright and dragged her to the main cabin area. Nick hauled Seattle into the shack.

"Take her to the barn and get it set up." Joe released her and grabbed Seattle's arm. "I'll bring the Injun."

She tried to make eye-contact with Seattle. A shiny reddish-brown substance trickled along his temple, coating the collar of his jacket. His head had a knot the size of a hockey puck on the left side. Joe's key method of abduction consisted of blunt force to the upper body. "Move forward, Injun, or I'll scalp you right here, right now."

Nick towed her from the cabin.

Inside the barn, McCartney evaluated the situation; the ending might be gruesome. Joe and Nick had gotten creative with a torture contraption meant to kill. Within minutes Nick wrapped her into a type of straitjacket, leaving the cocoon open at the top. He strung her from the rafters by a braided rope which burned into her wrists. Below her toes, a board rigged to a crossbow would fire. If her grip on the rope slipped, her feet would touch the board releasing an arrow. The harness kept her body aligned. She couldn't sway or swing her legs enough to clear the deadly trigger. Even if it were possible, her dismal upper body strength quickly faded.

"It's the terminator, a four-point tip on a steel shaft loaded onto a highly sensitive crossbow." Joe's smirk emphasized his recently fingernail-scratched face.

"Yeah, pointed right toward the red bull's eye," Nick goaded. He lifted his arm and pointed his gun fingers straight at her heart.

If she got out of this dilemma, she'd enlist in a weightlifting program. Maybe she'd ask Molly to go with her to a fitness center. Her weak arm muscles vibrated, bunched and jumped. Despite the frigid temperature, sweat beaded on her forehead. A couple of blinks helped to eliminate a sweaty droplet.

She tried to wrap the rope around one wrist but bungled the attempt and the pungent hemp grew slick. Her feet lightly brushed the wood. She moved her fingers higher and tightened her grip on the cord. How much longer could she last? *Stop, if I lose hope and my grip we'll die.*

"You're the biochemist, right? The one who impregnated Jennifer Picatelli?"

"Not true." Seattle stared at Mac. "Release her."

"The only way we're goin' to release her, is if you give us da' formula." Joe rubbed the knot on his chin, then reached into his pocket. He slowly withdrew a lighter and flicked it on and off. "This barn's old and dry, considering its winter and all. Probably one little flame and it'll be nothing but ashes in seconds." Joe let the lighter burn higher. Sparks flew out, landing on bits of straw.

Her hands slipped. She gasped. A clicking noise came from behind her. Damn, did they have a backup to trigger the release of the rope? Would she fall, die, in a matter of minutes?

An evil, gleeful smile appeared on Joe's face. "We want the formula. You've limited time. Start mixing the fuel. We'll test the formula and if it works then the sexy white will live."

"Let her go," Seattle whispered, "and I'll give you information."

She understood. Once again, the corrupted would win. Because of his integrity the formula and blueprint for saving the climate would be forfeited.

"No. Don't do it?" She screamed, making her palms slick with sweat. Her fingers cramped. A foot grazed the board. She hoisted her feet, crossing her ankles.

Seattle nodded to her. "I'll give it to you."

"Nick, let her go," Joe ordered.

Nick scuttled to the wall and unwound the rope from the hook on the stud. The pulley system swung her back from the board, banging her into the post. She landed on the solid ground and crumbled. In a fetal position, her legs were the first to recover. She rolled to her knees. Electricity jettisoned throughout her body as she twisted, trying to get free of the harness.

Joe extracted a switchblade from his pocket and proceeded to clean his fingernails. "If you didn't notice there's only one way out, which has a system in place. You so much as move toward the door, guaranteed, you'll both die."

"I need to take care 'some business. On the table are chemicals that Picatelli told us you would use. Don't bother trying to disarm the device, it's sensitive. Write fast Injun. We've another torture method in mind for your blonde squaw." He snorted. "Make sure the formula will fly."

"Yep, booby trap." Nick winked at her, as he sliced through the cord securing Seattle's hands. The blade clicked and retracted back inside its evil shell. "Here is a tablet, no internet, so don't think of being creative. I'll be back in New York minute."

The two men walked out of the barn. She closed her eyes, trying to absorb the pain and mental agony. Seattle was beside her in seconds. "It'll be okay. Rob's outside. He'll get us out of this." He removed the braided rope from her wrist and unfastened the straitjacket.

She tried to swallow, but her throat was dry and sore. A simple nod was all she could produce. Emotional pain ripped through her, she'd let him and his tribe down.

"Are you able to stand?" He waved a finger, bent over and dry heaved. Upright again, he took deep breaths. "Concussion."

"Yes." She pressed her hands to the ground and pushed to a stand. Her jeans and sweater drenched in icy moisture made her skin clammy. Her teeth chattered like a wind-up novelty store toy. "What can I do?"

Seattle removed his jacket and wrapped her in the warm softness. "Come. I'll create a fake formula." He winked.

She sank onto the floor. Seattle eased onto the chair and typed.

She closed her eyes. A second passed. Upon waking, she stood and ran the perimeter peering into the dark corners. *Seattle isn't here.* There wasn't evidence of a struggle. Had she been drugged or poisoned? Was that why the rope was slick?

Creak. Scratch. Creak. Scratch. Someone was prying the door. She didn't hesitate and ran to the crossbow. Why couldn't she have used a crossbow in one of her screenplays? It looked easy enough to use, set on a block of wood on top of five pieces of timber that resembled two inverted Vs with a crossbar to tie it together. How to aim and shoot the arrow?

She dragged the trip rope to the end of the arrow and threw the remaining coil in front. She shrugged off Seattle's jacket, sat on the ground between the horse legs and looked underneath. Standing again, she aligned the trigger, easy enough, now what was used to activate the arrow? At the whoosh of air, she placed an index finger on the narrow bar at the bottom and waited. A shard of moon as transparent as a thin sheet of silvery frost lit the area. Shadows distorted his face, but she recognized the firm jaw.

Chapter 20

"Rob?"

"Mac," Rob's gruff tone spanned the distance. "You, okay?"

She loosened her finger from the release trigger, then gripped the edge of the block of wood that held the crossbow. Her body shook, her knees felt like rubber and her aching arms spasmed. He rushed to her and pried her white-knuckled hands from the board.

Snuggled into the security of his warm arms she whispered, "I knew if you were alive, you'd come." She arched. "Wait, they said a booby-trap was attached to the door."

"They lied."

She coughed; her throat was parched and tender. She didn't have enough fluids to shed a tear, and she wanted to cry. Cry with relief that he was safe. Cry with happiness, because they would survive.

He touched her cheek. "Who did that to you?" His stance was tight, hands fisted at his sides.

"Where's Seattle?" She tugged his hand. "We need to leave before they come back."

The door slid open and bounced against the frame. Bitter icy wind blew in Joe and Nick. Joe tossed a cigarette to the floor and used his foot to dig it deep into the ground. By the lack of their expressions, finding Rob inside the barn hadn't surprised them.

"Well, the boys keep showing up, don't they? Nick, we don't have to worry about the cops finding us. They'll just end up in the barn, and we'll have them trapped."

"Unlike you, thieves who strike and run," Mac said.

"Shh." Rob dropped her hand and shoved her behind him.

"Lover boy and porn queen, together again." Joe spat onto the ground. "The Injun didn't want to play nice." He stomped the snow from his leather ankle boots. "Go get the chief, and I'll decide if we want to use the bitch or the stud."

Several minutes later, Nick dragged Seattle into the barn. Blood dripped from his newly battered head. His right knee and ankle went in opposite directions.

The rope, from the arrow contraption, tripped Nick. He bumped into Joe, and both lost their balance.

"Mac drop," Rob shouted. She scurried under the table. "Rob, the short one has a switchblade. The other one has a 9mm and a piece in a shoulder holster."

Luke dominated the entry, shotgun in hand, his face barely visible inside a fur lined hood.

Seattle remained unconscious. Joe threw the switchblade. Rob positioned himself behind the crossbow, pulled the trigger and launched the arrow. The four-sided-steel spear made a direct hit between Joe's shoulder and chest. Nick drew his 9mm synchronous with Luke pulling the trigger on the shotgun.

Nick's crimson gushers splattered blood across his chest, gravity took the gun, and he crumbled to the ground.

Luke reloaded the shotgun. Mac stood. Good God. If the arrow hadn't hit Joe, Luke would be dead. Rob ran forward and retrieved the equalizer from the ground.

"Dad, guard the door. Two here, are there any in the cabin?" He pivoted. She had one hand on the table, and one arm across her waist. "Mac?" he shouted.

Stunned, she stared at him.

"You've come too far to lose it now." His quiet calm voice cut through the muddle, and she moved.

"Maybe a third. I don't know if he's here." She grabbed a piece of the rope and tied a loop around Joe's wrists. "Too many movies show an assailant seemingly out, yet they attack later."

Luke whistled. "What kind of knot is that?"

"Double figure-of-eight loop, used by climbers. Not an easy knot to tie. I don't think any of these idiots would have a clue how to get out of it." She finished the knot and stood. "Is Nick dead?"

"Yes. Straight through the heart." Luke glanced around the barn.

"What about Seattle?" She leaned and spit.

Rob felt for a pulse. "Steady, but his leg is obviously broken."

At her stress limit, she bit her lip to keep from sobbing. It was all too much.

"Dad, did you drive here?"

Luke smiled. "Yes, parked a quarter of a mile down the road."

Mac sighed. Rob called Luke *Dad*, at least something positive came from the kidnapping.

"Get the car. Mac and I'll secure Seattle's leg."

"I drove a snowmobile. Easy to maneuver through the forest."

"Go." She glanced at Seattle. "I can fix the brace on his leg."

"Okay, Dad and I will get his snowmobile and the

horses we rode." He held both of her arms and looked into her eyes. "Get a straight narrow board, it'll go easier on him if he remains unconscious during the tie down."

She nodded.

"You can do this."

Numbly, she exhaled. A long piece of discarded metal acted as the lever to pry the board from the pedestal. A significant length of rope remained attached. She laid the plank beside Seattle, then went to Joe and removed car keys and a silk cloth from his trouser pocket.

Next, she fished around in Nick's pockets but didn't find anything of value. She picked up Seattle's discarded coat and draped it over him. She wrapped the silk cloth around nails on one end of the board and with shaking hands unfastened her bra. Under her sweater she pulled one shoulder strap down and over her hand, then snagged the other strap and drew the bra through the other sleeve. Seconds later she had the second set of sharp spikes covered. She eased the piece of wood under his broken leg. His pale face blanched, hopefully he'd remain unconscious. She gently twisted the rope around his leg and under the board, then secured the knot.

She started to rise, from her kneeled position, when he caught her hand. He hadn't made a sound while she worked on his leg. She lowered and smoothed his raven hair. "Seattle. I'm sorry. I'm so sorry that I had to hurt you. We'll get you to the hospital."

"I have to tell you." His voice sounded like a nail file grating over a crooked fingernail. He licked his lips.

"Shh. Save your strength." His mouth was hot to touch; she moved her hand to his forehead. "It'll be a grueling ride down the mountain. I'm going to check on

Rob and Luke. I'll be right back." She untangled her legs and ran to the door.

She grabbed a lamp and searched the darkness. "Rob! Luke!"

A fierce wind struck her. She dashed to the cabin, flung the door wide so the light would illuminate the space, and grabbed a blanket from a chair and a bottle of water from a table. The car had been parked in front of the cabin earlier. Where was it? Taken by the unknown person? Snowdrifts got deeper, while hail clung to her wet sweater like confetti. She trudged around the back of the barn and there it was.

She climbed onto the driver's seat and inserted the key into the ignition. It didn't start. She got out, ran around to the engine, opened the hood and placed the lantern on the fender. Thank you, Dad, for the boring minor car repair lessons. The spark plugs were disconnected, easy enough to fix. Back inside the jalopy, the motor came to life, and she slowly drove around to the front of the barn. The dashboard monitors indicated one half tank of gas. How much would it take to get to the hospital?

She backed through the open barn door, getting as close to Seattle as possible. Car parked, she exited and knelt beside him. "Tell me the best way to get you inside."

His feverish eyes looked darker and larger. "Move the passenger seat back, then roll me over to my good side."

She opened the door, pushed the seat in the last position. Beside Seattle again, she turned him onto his undamaged side, arranging the plank in the process. "Ready?"

"Yes."

She wedged her arm under his shoulder. He stood as straight as possible with his braced leg at a bent angle. Heavy warm breaths frosted the air. "A couple of steps."

His grip tightened around her shoulders. Astonished her smaller frame held his unwieldy mass, they lumbered along the solid ground with the cumbersome board dragging at his side. She blew out a breath. "Just a few more inches. Up and drop."

He closed his eyes, placed his hands on the seat, sat down and pushed with amazing strength. She put one knee on the car's floor and arranged the broken leg to rest on the edge. Chills racked his body, but he didn't utter a sound. She tucked the blanket around him and slid the water bottle between his arm and side. She admired him, she would have been screaming by this time or if lucky—passed out.

With great care she shut the door, climbed behind the steering wheel and put the car into drive. Heat on full blast, she positioned the fans toward him. Within minutes the chilled air warmed. She parked in front of the cabin, ran into the building and grabbed a plastic food bag. Outside, she filled the sack with snow and slid onto the driver's seat. She put her hand on his forehead. Volcano hot. She arranged the ice bag on his leg and opened the bottle of water. "Drink."

Where were they? She couldn't wait any longer.

Chapter 21

"Listen, horses causing a ruckus," Luke said.

"Let's go." The horses had been silent up to this time, and Rob could barely hear them now, but his father had a fox's hearing ability, sharp and sensitive. He led the way along a boot-printed path to where they'd hobbled the equine. "Shit, the Appaloosa is missing."

"I'll get the snowmobile. You take the horse to the barn and start the criminal's car." Luke hesitated. "I messed with their sparkplugs."

"You come with me, and we'll get the snowmobile later."

They led the black horse, until the lights of the car idling in front of the cabin lit the area. Rob held up his hand five fingers pressed together palm flat to stop the communication. Luke took the reins of the equine. Rob skulked, staying low and peered into the dark tinted windows of the vehicle.

The driver's side window, open a few inches, allowed soft rock to escape. Blonde locks were visible through the crack. He tapped lightly on the glass. She jerked and unlocked the doors. He eased the door open, and she rocketed into his arms. Taking a step back, he regained his balance.

"I'm so glad to see you. I was afraid." Mac glanced at Seattle. "We need to go."

"Seattle?"

"He has a fever, and his leg's swelling." Situated on the backseat, she leaned forward and repositioned the snow-filled bag on Seattle's temple.

Rob let out a loud whistle, then sat behind the steering wheel. Luke came out from behind the cabin, leading Devil. He sheltered the horse inside the barn, then climbed onto the backseat beside Mac and slammed the door.

The vehicle shot forward as Rob touched the pedal to the floorboard. The car slid sideways. He straightened the wheels, and they slid to the left.

Mac gripped Seattle's shoulders. "Slow down, I don't think I can keep him upright if we keep shifting." She moved the melting bag of snow to his leg.

"Icy dirt roads." Rob headed down the mountain. He handed his cellphone to Luke. "When we're close to a tower call the sheriff. Tell him about the kidnapper being bound and one's dead."

A few minutes later, Luke gave detailed descriptions and the names, as Mac provided them, to the police.

"Mac, it looks like you have exciting scenes to add to your screenplay," Luke said.

"Yes, it should be suspenseful." She held Seattle's hand, reassuring him they'd protect him.

One and a half hours later they arrived at the hospital. Seattle immediately went into surgery. Rob and Mac's beds were side by side in the emergency room, the curtain separating them had been pushed to the side. Luke remained in the lobby, cellphone in hand.

"There, there, honey bear, we'll get ya all fixed up now." The older white-haired nurse stated while placing sterile bandages over his ten stitches. With gentleness, she taped the gauze into place.

The doctor at Mac's bedside examined her injuries. "It appears as if you were banged up a bit. Quite a nice bundle of bruises. We'll get X-rays to determine if you've broken bones." Dr. Sam Das murmured while pressing his soft fingers onto her sensitive face. "There's no need for stitches. We'll butterfly the broken skin, and you'll have less scarring that way." He slathered a topical numbing solution on top and around the wounds, roughly cleaned them, then applied the bandages. "Hold this cold compress to your face." He nodded to a person dressed in scrubs. "Off to X-ray."

An hour later Dr. Das came to her side. "You're very lucky. No broken bones." He glanced at her wrists. "Apply a cold compress to your wrists. If you notice more swelling contact my office, if not return for follow up in a week."

She nodded and glanced into the mirror above the sterile aluminum sink. Rob came to stand behind her. Together, they looked like a pair of accident victims. He hugged her close and kissed her. "Come on, love. Let's go home."

"Okay, honey bear, but first I want to check on Seattle."

As she anticipated, he guffawed, then grimaced in pain. "Oops, no laughter until we're healed."

The village council must have been advised of Seattle's admittance because two of the elderly councilmen, Jennifer Picatelli, and an older version of Seattle were clustered in a group. The hustling of the medical staff and the silent tears of family members waiting in the emergency room didn't distract their focus. Each one kept a watchful eye on the surgery ward door.

"Dr. Coyote, I'm McCartney James. I was one of the people with Seattle when he was injured." She extended her hand. Rob's arm remained secure around her waist. A staff person, wearing a vivid pink uniform, shouted for Rob. He hesitated, then walked to the desk.

"Injured, is that what you're calling it? According to Jennifer he was kidnapped, because of a false belief he needed to save you." Dr. Coyote scratched his head, while keeping his glance toward the surgery room door and every white coat who exited. Worry-lines etched his face.

"Yes. I guess he was captured because of me. I'm sorry. He's a loyal, honest and brave man. I'm honored to have him as my friend." She sensed Rob's essence, before she saw him. He braided her fingers with his.

"Dr. Coyote, meet Rob Barringer, he saved Seattle's life." Mac glanced at Rob and attempted a smile.

"Rob, I cannot express my gratitude."

Rob withdrew keys from his pocket. "Call my house if you need anything. If Seattle needs anything. It's been a difficult couple of days." He speared Jennifer with a glance. "Ms. Picatelli, your father has been arrested because of his participation in the kidnapping. I suggest you tell Dr. Coyote and the council the truth about your involvement before Seattle does."

Jennifer's face paled. She'd made poor decisions to gain Seattle's favor. As Mac stared at her, sympathy left, and anger took over. All of them, Rob, Luke and Seattle could have lost their lives.

Dr. Coyote glanced at Jennifer. "Sure, Rob. Thanks."

Mac tightened her grip on his hand. They walked through the double electric doors and into the parking lot.

In Nick and Joe's car, she fastened the seatbelt. "Should we be driving this car? Isn't it evidence?"

"Probably not. Seattle told me his father had returned from Brazil. The country had created a substitute gas, ethanol, from sugar cane. He must've gone to the village and was told Seattle was in the hospital." Rob increased the heat. He stopped at a traffic light and turned toward her. "Will you marry me, Mac?"

"I had hoped to hear a four-letter word, before the five-letter word." She lightly touched his forehead, the white bandage glowed in the early daylight.

"Hum, I've been up for forty-eight hours, received ten stitches in my scalp, and you want me to figure out a word puzzle."

"L-o-v-e before m-a-r-r-y."

His frown spread into a grin, and then a full-fledged teeth-showing smile. "McCartney James, you're totally unpredictable. Your generosity towards others keeps you on a fast track to heaven. Your smart mouth helps to balance the saintliness: I want to spend the rest of my days on earth with you. I l-o-v-e you."

"You're the sweetest. I love you too, Rob. I'll marry you on one condition."

He frowned. "What condition?"

"I will marry you, but not a church wedding. I've a fear. Please understand. The only other man I wanted to marry was killed on the way to the church. Could we have a private ceremony at one of our houses?"

"Sure, family, a few friends and my minister will be fine." His kissed her, sealing the vow.

"Now that was a real kiss."

He chuckled. "Ouch."

"I'm glad you and Luke have reconciled."

"Yes."

"What did Return to Mother Earth mean? I'm sorry to upset you with the reminder. They picked up Lee Snyder. He's probably been extradited to New York. He wrote the phrase on your wall, right?"

She leaned her head against the seat's headrest.

"Yes, more than likely he was responsible. It's a phrase from Red Hot. When I researched the bibliography about the first activist named Forest Dog, one of his most devote beliefs concerned Mother Earth. He, rightfully, had been concerned about how people were treating earth and the imbalance of the ecology. The Native American's have a legend or more like a religion I guess that nature should always be in balance. Life has been created and maintained by Mother Earth. We evolved from nature, earth, and by the rights of balance we should return to the mother, red earth. In Red Hot, the hero and heroine had difficulty ah, developing their relationship because of their different backgrounds. One wealthy, from an elitist family, and one poor, a half-breed living on a reservation. One believed in using and discarding, and the other in ecology and balance."

"And I assume they get together. Why would Snyder write in red ink, Return to Mother Earth? The odd couple or rather the couple of opposites communicated." He wiggled his eyebrows.

She chuckled, making her throat hurt. "Yes, sexually. They also shared their beliefs and thoughts of the future. A future they wanted to share."

"And?"

"Ironically their destiny was like Water Star and Sam. Their families didn't approve of the union. They were successful and forced the couple to separate. Hawk, the man, was arrested for trespassing. He, like Forest Dog, marched in protest the injustices and inequalities for Native Americans. Due to prior arrest, Hawk went to jail. A deal was made with the DA to forego his jail-time, and he took refuge on the reservation. He was on probation and had to remain on the land. The woman, Paige, wasted away because of heart break. Her heart just stopped."

He snorted.

"Literally. The doctors declared cause of death heart failure due to depression or a broken heart. Hawk and his best friend stole her body from the funeral home. Each day Hawk would visit Paige's resting place at a hidden location on the reservation. He died an old man and was finally laid to rest near his soul mate. They both existed because of Mother Earth and together returned to Mother Earth." Mac took a long drink from Seattle's water bottle.

"You want me to believe this man broke into a funeral home and stole a body?" He all but tsked at the end of the question.

"It happens. He had a friend who cleaned the place. Hawk didn't take the entire chemical laden body, but rather her ashes. He went prepared with ashes from his fire pit. Transferring Paige's remains into a Munsi created earthen ware pottery. He left the fireplace ashes in the solid gold-urn her family had purchased."

"That's certainly more believable." He clasped her hand. "So, he thought you were meant to be together, ashes to ashes. He intended to kill you."

"I hope they put him away for a very long time." She rubbed the hard pads of his hand with her fingers.

"They will. I love you, Mac. I plan to tell you often."

She lifted his hand and kissed the bruised knuckles. "After we rest awhile, do you want to get my heart pumping strong and fast?"

Rob grinned at her. "I know exercises that'll do that."

Chapter 22

Rob met Dr. Caleb Coyote at the entrance of the village. The sun shone on the land, creating an aura of serenity hazing the pall of the previous few days. He shut off the truck's motor, grabbed his father's shotgun and a few shells. He nodded a greeting to Caleb as he slid the bullets into his coat pocket. The scent of ceremonial smoke reminded him of the sensitivity of the situation. An outsider, in a protected environment, he was surrounded by a strong tightly knit group.

"Rob." Caleb's serious expression wouldn't change his mind.

"Caleb. Did you tell the council?"

"Yes. They understand your wish to speak to him. The confidentiality we spoke about is confirmed."

"How's Seattle today?" Rob walked toward the house.

Dr. Coyote followed. "He's doing well. As I told you on the phone, I talked to Jennifer and the other council members to get an accurate picture." Caleb pointed toward the rifle. "I don't believe you'll need the gun."

"He's very clever, and I'm not taking chances with my family." Rob clutched the weapon, refusing to relinquish the power. Determined to get restitution, he wouldn't leave before he got what he wanted.

"You're on private property. He's a member of our

tribe, and he'll be punished according to our policies and legal system," Dr. Coyote stated in a firm voice.

They arrived at the house. Rob knocked. With no response he glanced at Caleb, then turned the knob and as expected found it locked. He'd hoped for the element of total surprise.

"As you said, 'he's very clever'," Caleb said laconically. His eyes glittered behind the horn-rimmed glasses.

With a scowl, Rob slammed his fist against the solid maple. A sleepy-eyed Caedmon Star opened the door and tried to slam it shut, but Rob slid the rifle between the seal and the frame. A push and the door hit hard on the wall. Caedmon sprinted. Rob caught him at the back door, grabbed the collar of the young man's shirt and jerked him into the kitchen.

"It's over Caedmon." Caleb released a sigh.

Caedmon's shoulders slumped forward, his chin hit his chest, and his fists relaxed at his sides. Like a trapped rat he surrendered, then dropped onto a metal chair.

Caleb removed his cellphone and dialed. "We have him. Affirmative. Give us a few minutes to discuss details. Right."

"Caedmon you are, of course, surrounded by your own people. People whom you betrayed. You need to sing a truthful song to please Rob and me." Dr. Coyote sat and leaned against the rails of the chair. "From what you tell us, I'll either support you at council trial or help to prosecute."

Rob slipped the rifle sling over his shoulder and straddled a mission style chair facing Caedmon.

Caedmon ran his hands over his face and stood. Rob shoved him onto the chair. "I need a drink. Juice is in fridge." Caedmon removed his glasses and wiped them with the end of his t-shirt.

Caleb handed the carton to the suspected traitor, who swallowed half of the contents. He glanced at Rob. "How did you find out?"

"An email." Rob removed his cellphone from the inside pocket of his jacket. "Do I need to read it to you, to refresh your memory?"

"No. It's clear in my mind," Caedmon answered.

"I guess you better start at the beginning," Rob demanded.

"I met her in Lantern a few weeks after the Carpenter house sold. She was wandering around the streets looking in the shop windows, and she literally stole my breath. I stood there with my mouth open and my hand on my chest trying to physically pump air back into my lungs. She asked if she could help me, get a med tech, anything. I told her if she spent the rest of her life with me, I'd survive." Caedmon had an absent-minded expression.

Caleb snorted, but Rob understood. "Continue." He filled a cup with water and sat.

"I showed her the town. It's beautiful when you look at it with fresh sight. We spent an hour together, and I knew I would do anything for her. We exchanged social media information and addresses. As Shakespeare wrote 'Thou art a votary to fond desire.' " Caedmon twisted his hands together, as if in embarrassment.

"You're not in Verona now, although your love was paralyzing and self-pitying. Whose idea was it to kidnap Mac?" Rob had to know. The man's story would impact how he'd proceed.

"Mine." Caedmon must have realized how quickly

he responded because he locked glances with Rob and restated, "It was my idea. She wasn't supposed to get hurt. No one was supposed to get hurt."

"My son is in critical condition," Caleb growled.

"Why her?" Rob asked.

"Seattle. He'd do anything for her. Since old Dr. Coyote was out of the country, he was the only one who knew the exact formula." He sighed. "Jennifer was the stumbling block. I approached her, and we came to an understanding." He swirled the dregs of the juice around in the container.

"Explain," Caleb insisted.

"Jennifer wanted Seattle. She thought that if she had money, she could buy things, get a nice haircut, expensive perfume, and convince him to want her. But Seattle wanted Mac. Mac wanted Rob. Rob was a reluctant suitor."

A scowl formed on Caleb's face. "Get to the point, Caedmon."

"Don't get me wrong, he's a brilliant biochemist and his appearance alone would get him any girl, but the man cannot talk to women. Jennifer swooped in and offered her help. She was his human dating guide, including consummation." Caedmon nodded to Dr. Coyote. "She lied to him; by the way, she's not pregnant."

"Enough. Get to the point." Rob wasn't willing to listen to his fiancée be discussed as a goal for another man.

"Jennifer's father was having an affair with Liza Carpenter," Caedmon said.

Caleb coughed, a "don't say anything else" cough.

"I know, it made me want to puke also. She was staying with her Belduchi relatives in New Jersey. She'd lost all her money, from the sale of her house, by gambling in Atlantic City. She was desperate." Caedmon glanced at Caleb with an expression of a naughty child instead of a man. "We all needed money for a variety of reasons. We would've given the credit to you, Seattle, and the others but we needed the money."

"I understand Liza's gambling, Picatelli's drinking, Jennifer's desire for something better, but what I don't understand is why you wanted the money?" Dr. Coyote's voice was harsh and full of bitterness. The village had been betrayed by three of their own, and they would not take the treachery lightly.

"Love for a woman who expected to be treated like a princess, given constant attention and elegance in her lifestyle," Caedmon said.

Rob stiffened in his seat. He didn't want Caedmon to reveal Cassie's name. Although she shared the guilt, she was family, and he'd protect her until the truth needed to be revealed.

"New York's a very expensive place to live. I wanted to start a new life with my love. I couldn't do that without a source of income and a solid base."

"Who's the girl?" Caleb asked.

"Is that why you agreed to study and pass the bar exams?" Rob asked before Caedmon could answer.

"Yes. The girl is—"

"And why you chose New York as your practice exam?" Rob interrupted.

"Yes." Caedmon bowed his head in shame.

"So, you never intended to take the Indiana Bar. You never intended to help your people?" Rob wanted to divert the attention away from Cassie and focus on Caedmon's wrongdoing.

"No."

"Enough. I've heard enough. Caedmon you'll be under house arrest. Guards will be posted. I'll talk with the council." Caleb abruptly stood. "Fortunately, no one was killed. I assume you had nothing to do with Darrell Carpenter's death?"

"No." Caedmon's hands were now holding his head up. "Did the police get Liza's relatives?"

"Yes," Caleb and Rob answered simultaneously.

"The formula's safe then?" Caedmon whispered.

"Yes. Seattle gave a false formula. Ironically, one of them was a chemical specialist and knew the ingredients were bogus." Caleb hesitated. "Communication or not, it is evident my half-breed son has more integrity than the other three nation members involved. He wouldn't disclose the formula and as a result has a room in intensive care."

"Yes. May I write a letter to her."

Rob flashed him a dark scowl.

"My girl? I want to explain why I wouldn't be able to see her again," Caedmon said.

"You can write it from prison," Caleb answered as he walked away.

Rob followed Caleb from the house. A guard assumed a position in front of the misguided suitor's door.

He climbed into the truck, shoved the rifle onto the floor, and rolled down the window.

"I haven't met Mac's daughter, but the pieces fit." Dr. Coyote rubbed an index finger on the side his nose. "So, you know?"

"Yes," Rob said.

"She knew about the tutoring, the formula and

betrayed her own mother. Cassie sounds like a spoiled child, but she's your responsibility now. We'll proceed with litigation against Caedmon and the two Picatelli. I'll keep Cassandra's name out of it. The tribe respects Mac and will honor her. The sins of the children should not haunt the parents." Caleb pushed his fist against Rob's arm. "You must decide what to do about the girl."

"Tell Mac or to deal with Cassie alone?" Rob asked.

"Yes, my friend. You must decide how to deal with your tribe as you see fit." Caleb had the audacity to smile.

"Right, Mac." Would their developing relationship be strong enough to handle this magnitude of betrayal? Either the information would bring them closer together or separate them forever. Unfortunately, he didn't have a choice. He rubbed his uninjured temple.

"Do you want me to go with you to explain the possible outcomes for Caedmon?" Caleb asked.

Rob shook his head. "No, I'm the head of the family. It's my responsibility."

****

Rob rang the doorbell, then the barking commenced.

"Move. No, stay." She opened the door, revealing Scat's huge feet as he stood waist high snug between Mac and the wall. His fiancée was breathtaking. Dressed in jogging clothes, with her hair in a loose ponytail, she reminded him of the first time they'd met.

"Hi." She kissed him quick as if kissing him was a habit, a pattern for the rest of their lives.

"Hi." He touched her chin. "The swelling is down, and the bruises are darker."

"They'll heal. We need to work on the puppy training again. For some reason Scat has developed new bad habits." She tugged his collar. "Sit."

"Scat. Down." His calm monotone voice prompted the dog to plop his rear onto the floor.

"Nice." She grabbed Rob's hand and drew him toward the bedroom. "I want you to look at some dress options for the wedding. Molly helped me narrow it down to three choices. Fortunately, Psycho Snyder didn't go into the guest room closet to shred clothing, which is where I store the good clothes." She released his hand. "Sit."

Rob dropped onto the nearest chair. "Is Cassie here?"

"No. She went with Marcus to the market to restock the refrigerator." She held up three gowns, took a brown dress and held it in front of her. Rejected, she hung it on a doorknob. A white garment, full in the skirt was sported and latched over the top of the first. Finally, she held out a pale blue dress with ruffles around the neck and hem.

"Okay, from your expression I can rule out the blue. What about the white or champagne?" she asked.

"I like the first one. It reminds me of moonshine and that was a memorable evening." The tinkling of her laugh brought chills to his skin. He hoped she would still want to laugh, with him, in a few minutes.

She held the dress tight to her body and twisted from side to side in front of the full-length mirror. He walked behind her and met her glance in their reflections. The instant she saw the truth; she turned into his arms and drew his mouth down for a long hard kiss. A kiss laced with desperation. It had taken them so long to find this thing they shared—love. Could real love conquer all?

"Mac, we need to talk," he whispered.

"I know." She sighed.

From inside his jacket pocket, Rob withdrew a copy of the letter Caedmon sent to Cassie. Mac walked to the bedside table and removed two pieces of paper. Glassy eyed she extended a parchment exposing an email address to Cassandra James.

"I found the letters when Molly and I were cleaning earlier today."

"Does she know?" Rob asked. "Molly?"

"No," she whispered.

He nodded. "Caedmon is culpable, and he will go before the Coterie council. He'll be tried for his actions and the results of those actions. Dr. Caleb Coyote will try to keep Cassie's name out of it. The Picatelli will also be dealt with." Rob sighed. "What do you want to do?"

"First instinct, forget it ever happened. But maybe that's why it did happen. I never addressed bad behavior. I ignored the small things. Rob, my daughter hates me."

He led her to the bed and sat on the edge, pulled her onto his lap and rubbed soothing circles on her back. "She doesn't hate you. Cassie realized you were beginning a new life. A life, in which she wasn't the focus." God, his heart ached for her. From personal experience, he understood how betrayal shook a person's world.

"Pe—pep—people were hurt. You. Seattle. Because she didn't consider the consequences, people were hurt." She inhaled.

"Mac, the swelling will come back, and you'll have the stinging return."

"Tell me what to do." She pulled her sleeve over her hand and dabbed her face.

"Only you can make that decision. I'm here for you, to listen and not judge. I'll be your rock."

Chapter 23

"Screaming bullets, flying fists, and the big showdown, doesn't have any comparison to you, my heart, my husband." Mac touched his chest and drew small circles around his peaked nipples. She had the bruised side of her face against the pillow, the unblemished side exposed. In the past few weeks, the marring had faded to the point that make-up covered the remaining yellow spots. However, they'd taken a sensual shower, and the cosmetics went down the drain.

"I have to admit, it keeps getting better." He stilled her hand. "I think the ceremony went very well. Don't you?"

"Yes. Lovely." She touched his scarred head. The stitches had been removed. "We're both scarred now."

He smoothed the ridges of her scar. "Yes. We both have scars, but they won't exist if we don't let them."

"Invisible scars." She cleared her throat. "Thanks for helping me get Cassie settled at the university. Xavier and Noah are transporting her belongings to her dorm room. Do you think she'll adjust?"

"Yes. I think the move and the counseling will help." Rob kissed her soft and quick.

"What about the community service at the village? Seattle's idea, and I think it's a good one. I'm not sure about three years though." She blew out a puff of air. "It's only on breaks and during the summer, tutoring kids and acquainting them with the arts. He suffered the most. Is she being held accountable?"

He tapped her hand, resting on his chest. "She'll help others and be close enough to see you. Speaking of others, Xavier brought a copy of Red Hot. I watched the movie last night after the bachelor party. It was like cascading water over a hot body. It feels refreshing and satisfying while it envelops you, but when it stops the burn is back. You create a need, making satisfaction unobtainable."

"Thank you." She stuffed covers under her arms. "That's quite the review."

"The story's amazing."

"Why?" She stared at him.

"Because it's based on the truth."

Maybe she was fishing for compliments. He knew her quirks, her biting, sometimes condescending humor and her work ethics. By marrying her, he loved her despite those few negatives. She honestly wanted to know what he thought. Her gaze didn't waver from his.

"And because my beautiful intelligent wife made a depressing story come to life. The narrative could have been mundane, and no one would have thought twice about it. You created a memorable expose. I understand why the village council convinced you to help them. You've a sincere empathy for the Native Americans." He kissed her, more of a peck on her lips. "I'm very proud of you. Let's talk about a new aka or alias or whatever you call it."

"New name? What, you're tired of Mac Barringer already? It's only been ten hours?"

"McCartney James was exposed to the public with the arrest of the New Jersey guys, the AP has captured our wedding photo, and we're probably already a meme. You're infamous, renowned, so your new name will be everywhere. What moniker do you want to create to write under?"

"What do you think happened to the third guy? The one who stole the speckled horse?

"We'll find him or her, as it could have been Liza Carpenter." He sighed. "I never want to feel that way again. Helpless. Powerless. Fearful of what could happen to you."

"My hero, my husband." She lifted the covers and pushed her naked body flush against his. "Changing my name isn't going to prevent a crazy from finding me. We both understand how critical it is to grab life and squeeze as much as possible out of it. Neither of us can prevent what tomorrow will hold."

"I'm all-in for seizing the day, Mrs. Barringer."

A word about the author…

jj inherited her name and creativity from her grandmother. John James McCartney, a Keller forefather, inspired this story. A love of literature and adventure takes jj to many wondrous places. Storytelling is her passion, an essential part of her world, and she wants to share the magic. Please enjoy pieces of her life through her tales.

@jjkellerauthor

https://romancewithjjkeller.wordpress.com

Thank you for purchasing
this publication of The Wild Rose Press, Inc.

For questions or more information
contact us at
info@thewildrosepress.com.

The Wild Rose Press, Inc.
www.thewildrosepress.com